FIC
HAU

CPS – MORRILL SCHOOL

W9-ATR-942

No place.

34880030013697

FIC
HAU

C.1

Haugaard, Kay.

No place.

34880030013697

$15.95

DATE			

CPS – MORRILL SCHOOL
CHICAGO PUBLIC SCHOOLS
6011 S ROCKWELL STREET
CHICAGO, IL 60629
12/15/2004

BAKER & TAYLOR

No Place

ALSO BY KAY HAUGAARD

Myeko's Gift

China Boy

No Place

Kay Haugaard

MILKWEED EDITIONS

FIC
HAU
C.1
2005
15.95

This novel was inspired by an actual class project, but the characters and events in this book are fictional. Any similarities to real persons, living or dead, are coincidental and not intended by the author.

© 1998, Text by Kay Haugaard
© 1998, Cover painting by Michelle Peterson-Albandoz
© 1998, Interior illustration by Luis Montenegro
All rights reserved. Except for brief quotations in critical articles or reviews, no part of this book may be reproduced in any manner without prior written permission from the publisher: Milkweed Editions, 430 First Avenue North, Suite 400, Minneapolis, MN 55401
Distributed by Publishers Group West

Published 1998 by Milkweed Editions
Printed in the United States of America
Cover design by Adrian Morgan, Red Letter Design
Cover painting by Michelle Peterson-Albandoz
Illustration on pg. vi by Luis Montenegro
The text of this book is set in Goudy Modern
98 99 00 01 02   5 4 3 2 1
First Edition

Milkweed Editions is a not-for-profit publisher. This book has been partially underwritten by the James R. Thorpe Foundation. We also gratefully acknowledge the support of Alliance for Reading funders: Cray Research, a Silicon Graphics Company; Dayton Hudson Circle of Giving; Ecolab Foundation; Musser Fund; Jay and Rose Phillips Foundation; Rathmann Family Foundation; Target Stores; United Arts School and Partnership Funds. Other support has been provided by the Elmer L. and Eleanor J. Andersen Foundation; James Ford Bell Foundation; Dayton's, Mervyn's, and Target Stores by the Dayton Hudson Foundation; Doherty, Rumble & Butler Foundation; Dorsey & Whitney Foundation; General Mills Foundation; Honeywell Foundation; Jerome Foundation; McKnight Foundation; Minnesota State Arts Board through an appropriation by the Minnesota State Legislature; Norwest Foundation on behalf of Norwest Bank Minnesota, Norwest Investment Management & Trust, Lowry Hill, Norwest Investment Services, Inc.; Lawrence and Elizabeth Ann O'Shaughnessy Charitable Income Trust in honor of Lawrence M. O'Shaughnessy; Oswald Family Foundation; Piper Jaffray Companies, Inc.; Ritz Foundation on behalf of Mr. and Mrs. E. J. Phelps Jr.; John and Beverly Rollwagen Fund of the Minneapolis Foundation; St. Paul Companies, Inc.; Star Tribune Foundation; and by the support of generous individuals.

Library of Congress Cataloging-in-Publication Data

Haugaard, Kay.
    No place / Kay Haugaard. — 1st ed.
      p. cm.
    Summary: Having no place to play in their run-down inner city Los Angeles neighborhood, twelve-year-old Arturo and the other students in his sixth-grade class raise money and build a park, in the process learning about hard work, creativity, and teamwork.
    ISBN 1-57131-616-7 (alk. paper). — ISBN 1-57131-617-5 (pbk. : alk. paper)
    [1. Parks—Fiction. 2. Moneymaking projects—Fiction. 3. Inner cities—Fiction.
4. City and town life—California—Los Angeles—Fiction. 5. Los Angeles (Calif.)—
Fiction. 6. Hispanic Americans—Fiction. I. Title.
PZ7.H2865No 1998
[Fic]—dc21   98-39980
                                                                 CIP
                                                                  AC

This book is printed on acid-free paper.

This book is dedicated to
Bob and Marian Wilson,
without whose generous help
it could not have been written.

No Place

CHAPTER 1

THE ROARING RIVER of morning traffic down the freeway near his apartment building was like an alarm clock for Arturo. It woke him for school at about seven every morning. By then Mama and Papa had already gone to work.

This morning Arturo pulled the quilt up around his ears. His big brother, Francisco, was yelling at one of the Lopez kids, "Hey, hurry up in there! It's our bathroom too, you know."

Mrs. Lopez yelled back at Francisco, in Spanish, that they were paying rent, too. If he didn't like sharing the bathroom, she said, he should tell his papa to go find a fancy apartment with a private one—as if his papa could afford it.

Then the Lopez baby started to cry, and the bathroom door slammed. Who could sleep with such a racket? Arturo sat up and pulled his blue-and-white football shirt from his dresser drawer and started to get dressed.

While Arturo was tying his shoes, Francisco came into the bedroom. He was wearing a black bandanna tied around his head, a new plaid shirt, and baggy black pants. Arturo stared at him. He looked like one of *Los Vatos Locos.*

"Hey, Francisco, where did you get the sharp clothes?" Arturo looked down at his tennis shoes. The right one had a hole where his little toe stuck out. Mama had said she'd take him to get new ones at Buy-Rite. But whenever he asked her she said, maybe next Friday. That's when the women at Judy's Sportswear got paid.

Francisco was admiring himself in the cracked mirror

behind the *Virgen de Guadalupe* candle. Carefully, he ran his finger over his upper lip.

"Hey, Francisco, you're getting a moustache!"

Fine, black hairs were starting to form a line across Francisco's upper lip. "Hey, man, you look like Pancho Villa," Arturo laughed.

"Whattya mean, getting one? You just haven't noticed." Francisco lifted his chin proudly and stroked the almost invisible hairs as affectionately as if he were petting a prize bull.

Grabbing a comb from the dresser, Arturo smoothed down his straight, dark hair, which was standing up in clumps. "Hey, did Mama and Papa give you money for the clothes?" Arturo pulled down his jersey and stuck his finger into the biggest of three holes. "Why didn't they get some for me, too?"

"Never mind, *chico.*" Francisco rubbed Arturo's neatly combed hair into a tousled mess. "Just go on to school."

"Don't call me *chico* anymore. I'm not so little. I'm in sixth grade. I'm going to graduate from elementary school this year. Then I'll be in junior high like you!"

So he was kind of little. So what! Arturo suddenly thought of Clorissa, who was so tall that she could look down on him from way up. She must weigh twice as much as I do, Arturo thought. The fact that she was so much bigger than he was made Arturo mad—and she was just eleven years old. But Angel, his best friend, was even smaller than Arturo. That was good.

When they walked out into the kitchen, Arturo turned on the stove burner and grabbed a tortilla from the sack on the counter. "How old do you have to be to join *Los Vatos Locos*, Francisco?" Arturo smiled admiringly at his brother

4

while slapping the tortilla back and forth over the hot burner. Francisco looked so smooth, so suave. Those new shiny black shoes with the strap and buckle across the front were the greatest! Talk about sharp!

"A few more years, *chico.*" Francisco winked as he walked out the door.

"Hey, Francisco, aren't you going to school with me?"

"Nah, I've got more important things to do. Got to meet the guys down at the store. School is for *niños.*" Francisco walked out with a strut he had just started using. Turning, he pointed at Arturo. *"Chico,* don't tell Mama or Papa about my clothes, okay?"

Arturo scowled. *Niño! Chico!* Huh! But when Francisco called back, Arturo answered, "Okay, okay!" He scooped a big spoonful of mashed frijoles from a pot on the stove and spread it onto his warm tortilla, which he folded and then ate. That *hermano* of his! So school was just for babies! Ha! Francisco was only fourteen. Arturo was going to be twelve next month. Twelve wasn't so far from fourteen.

There was just one thing Arturo wanted: to join *Los Vatos Locos* so he could wear sharp new clothes and drive around in a low rider with the other guys. School was dumb and a waste of time, yet here he was starting another whole year of it.

Suddenly Arturo saw the time on the clock beside the calendar from St. Augustine's Church: September, just two weeks into the sixth grade. Nine months before he got out of elementary school. Arturo sighed. Mama would kill him if he skipped school. He hated having to do what adults told him to do.

Grabbing a can of cola from the refrigerator, he opened it and started for school. Once he joined the *Vatos,* nobody would tell him what to do.

5

CHAPTER 2

AS ARTURO STEPPED INTO the stairwell, he saw two of the Lopez kids and Maria's little sister playing on the stairs.

"Rrrrr, rrroom!" One little boy crawled along a stair pushing a blue-and-green plastic dump truck. "Rrrrr, rrroom." He pushed it slowly over Arturo's shoe as if he were driving over a mountain. Arturo took a gulp of his soda while the truck drove over.

"Hey, look out, *niño.*" Arturo moved his foot. Señora Lopez put her head out the door. "Be careful where you step; my *niños* don't have any other place to play."

"I was being careful." Arturo tiptoed down the steps, past the little girl holding her doll and the baby just sitting at the bottom.

As he started out the heavy, metal-barred door, a voice called from the Garcia's apartment. "Hey, Arturo! Wait a sec till I get my shoes on. I'll walk to school with you." Maria stood in her stocking feet at the top of the stairs.

What a pest! "Nah, it's already late." Arturo hurried on. Maria was always following him around. He wished she'd get lost.

Stepping out onto the sidewalk, he saw another Lopez kid, the four year old, across the street. He was playing in the body of an abandoned car. It had no wheels, the windows were broken, and the body was beaten in. The boy was sitting on bare seat springs. Tufts of stuffing lay on the floor. *Los Vatos Locos*—The Crazy Boys—and *El Lobo*—The

Wolf—were sprayed on the trunk. Arturo and Angel had done it last week when Angel's cousin—*El Lobo*, the head of the *Vatos*—came to visit and brought some spray paint. But what was that right above his and Angel's graffiti? Someone had sprayed, in purple, rounded gang-style printing, "33RD"—for the Thirty-third Street Gang. Arturo felt a stab of anger to see the name of the rivals of *Los Vatos Locos*.

"Arturo," the little boy said, pretending to turn the missing steering wheel. "Rmmmmm, brmmmmmm." He smiled proudly. *"Tengo un carro."*

"Yeah, you've got a car all right. You'll get hurt in that hunk of junk." There was broken glass on the floorboard. "Go on home, *niño!*" Arturo yelled. It felt good to call someone else a *niño*. Besides, he always got the Lopez kids' names mixed up. There were so many of them.

As he walked along, he thought about the purple "33RD" painted over the *Vatos* mark. It might mean trouble. He kicked a take-out fried-chicken box and stomped on a styrofoam cup with a straw sticking out the top as he continued down the sidewalk.

"Hola, Arturo." Angel ran toward him past the bleached, ragged hulk of an overturned couch. A little girl sat in the shade of the couch putting pieces of glass and rocks in lines.

Angel pulled a couple of cigarettes out of his pocket and handed them to Arturo. Arturo finished the last gulp of his cola and threw the can against a telephone pole. He took the cigarettes and slid them into his pocket.

"Did you see the 33RD mark over there?" Arturo pointed.

"Yeah! Looks like trouble!" Angel grinned excitedly.

A lighted cigarette hung from Angel's mouth. Dark

ringlets curled around his face, and his big, dark eyes looked as innocent as those of the little kid in the car. Arturo remembered what Father Miller had said when he asked Angel to be an altar boy. "You look just like your name, Angel. You could fool anyone."

Yeah, if those angels at St. Augustine's Church had black hair and brown eyes, they would look just like his buddy, Arturo thought.

Suddenly Arturo noticed movement behind the rusty skeleton of a truck cab by the barbwire-topped fence bordering the freeway. It was Francisco with one of the *Vatos*. He waved and yelled, "Hey, Francisco!" but his brother turned away as if avoiding him.

"Hey, man, I wonder what he doesn't want you to know?" Angel smirked at Arturo.

Arturo's cheeks got hot with anger and embarrassment. "He's busy talking to his *compañero*."

"Yeah, sure. My cousin told me about Francisco joining."

Now Arturo was really angry. Angel had known before he had! That Francisco sure thought he was hot snot!

"My cousin's going to get me in pretty soon." Angel smiled tauntingly.

Arturo didn't answer. Angel was always bragging about his cousin, *El Lobo*, about how much power he had as the leader of *Los Vatos Locos*. Arturo ignored Angel just as Francisco had ignored him and kept walking down La Luna Street.

Angel blew out a puff of smoke. "Hey, you want to ditch?"

"Nah, not today." Arturo was really annoyed with Angel and Francisco.

At the corner where they usually turned to go to school,

Arturo went on farther. He walked slowly by the ornamented black-iron fence in front of some fancy old homes. He looked through the fence at the tall, shady trees. There were orange and yellow flowers blooming along a walk.

Arturo found himself thinking about how great it would be to walk around inside the fenced area—maybe even to play. What a different world this was from La Luna. Sometimes Arturo got angry with La Luna. Sometimes he felt like running away from it.

"Man, what are you gawking at?" Angel finished his cigarette and ground the butt into the sidewalk.

Arturo trotted the rest of the way to school and collapsed into his seat as the bell rang. Maria Garcia leaned across the aisle and whispered, "Why didn't you wait for me?"

Angel, sitting over two rows, was watching and grinning his head off.

Arturo caught his breath and pushed his damp hair out of his eyes. Miss Fenwick, their teacher, was standing by her desk, and a young man he'd never seen was standing beside her.

Miss Fenwick was a pretty lady, Arturo thought, but she wore funny clothes. Today she had on a real baggy, long, blue-denim dress that came down almost to her flat, clunky sandals. She was so slim that the dress looked like it was made for someone twice as wide as she was. "Good morning, class. *Buenos días, clase.*" She had a very soft voice. Angel had said that her short blonde hair looked kind of like a toadstool, and as Arturo looked at her, he agreed.

"This is Edward Moreno, boys and girls." Miss Fenwick's smile seemed rather shy. "He is studying at the university to be a teacher and will be working with us a couple days a week. Tell us about your project, Mr. Moreno. And because a number of the boys and girls understand only Spanish, would you repeat what you say in Spanish, please?"

Mr. Moreno pulled his tall, slim body up straighter, and his smile brightened. "Okay!" He rubbed his hands together eagerly. "Let's start by talking about your community right here around Southwood Elementary School. What would make your community better?"

Mr. Moreno didn't have trouble repeating himself in Spanish. He spoke as though he had learned it when he was young. That surprised Arturo. Miss Fenwick didn't know much Spanish. Sometimes she had Arturo or another kid translate for her.

Everyone was really quiet for a minute. Juanita's eyes got big behind her glasses. Arturo looked at her. Everything about Juanita was tiny but her eyes. Pushing her glasses up her tiny nose, she spoke in a mouse-squeaky voice. "I think it's awful how people throw trash in the streets. There are waxed-paper Big Slurp cups and straws and french-fry containers and all kinds of junk. Yesterday I saw the Ochoa's little boy sitting on La Luna, playing with a fish head! I think we should pick up the trash."

Remembering the can he had thrown on the ground that morning, Arturo looked the other way.

"A fish head?" Mr. Moreno looked cool in his white shirt, his rolled-up sleeves, and his blue slacks. He sat on Miss Fenwick's desk with his long legs stretched out in front of him. Miss Fenwick pulled her chair to the side when she sat down so she could see around him.

"Where did he get a fish head?"

LeDru waved his chocolate brown arm vigorously. "There's lots of garbage in that dump by the freeway. One day I found a whole crate of rotten oranges there."

Clorissa's dark eyes were calm in her coffee-colored face as she considered the question. "Maybe we could help people paint their houses or their fences if they are too busy to do it themselves."

That was just like Clorissa, thought Arturo. Always full of noble ideas that no one would ever really do.

Miss Fenwick smoothed a strand of her hair. "I think those are wonderful ideas."

"We could even get some nails and hammers and stuff and help people fix fences and things," Trevor said from the back of the classroom.

Looking at him, Arturo thought that Trevor's white face and long, straight blond hair made him look like a loaf of unbaked bread among golden and brown ones.

"We could plant flowers." Maria smoothed her pink dress. "I like petunias. They have pretty colors."

Angel slumped way down in his desk with his eyes half closed. "That's not going to do any good," he sneered. "What this neighborhood needs is dynamite to blow it up, or a million dollars to move everyone away!"

Juanita sat up stiffly. "Oh, Angel, you never say anything good."

"I'm sure Angel meant that the neighborhood has real problems." Miss Fenwick lowered her brows as she looked at Angel.

"Yeah, and it wouldn't hurt to chase out the drug dealers either," said LeDru.

There was a really long silence. Then Mr. Moreno said, "Maybe we should let the police do that."

"For now, we all know how to say no," Miss Fenwick said with an encouraging smile.

Arturo hadn't said anything so far. He was still mad at

Angel. Suddenly he spoke up. "What we need is a park! Nobody has any place to play except in the street and on roofs."

The whole room burst into cheers and hand clapping. "Arturo's right. We need a park to play in. Then little kids won't have to play with fish heads," Juanita said enthusiastically.

Everyone laughed.

"A park would be wonderful for all the people." Clorissa pushed up the sleeves of her red sweatshirt. "But no one's going to make a park for us. And where could they even put a park?"

"Blow up a few old dumpy houses and make room!" Angel laughed wildly at his own remark.

"Yeah, like yours," said LeDru.

"Boys and girls!" Miss Fenwick tried to sound stern. "Let's be constructive."

"Not destructive," said Clorissa.

"But who would make a park for us? That takes a lot of money, even if we had some land. Who does that—the government?" Trevor wanted to know.

"These are wonderful questions, kids." Miss Fenwick lifted her eyebrows brightly.

"What a terrific group you are," Mr. Moreno said. "Now that we've thought of what this community needs, let's have fun thinking about what we can do to help. Each of you write down what you would like to have in a park and bring it to class on Monday."

"Then in art class we will make illustrations of what we'd like," Miss Fenwick added.

That afternoon as Angel and Arturo were walking home, Arturo thought about Mr. Moreno and the class discussion.

It was pretty dumb even to talk about creating a park. As they walked past the handbag factory, Arturo saw all the *cholo* writing of Francisco's gang on the white, upperpart of the building. Just below it, Arturo saw another purple 33RD tag. He didn't say anything, but it bothered him.

"Wanna go out tonight after supper?" Angel asked.

"Yeah, okay." Arturo answered, though he was thinking of other things.

"Meet you at the clubhouse," Angel said and waved as he left.

"Right." Arturo looked down and saw a styrofoam cup from Burger Heaven. There were weeds growing up beside it in the gutter. He jumped off the sidewalk and stomped on the cup with both feet. Then he walked off furiously with his hands thrust in his pockets. A park in this neighborhood? Nice? Sure! It would be nice to be a millionaire, too, and have a new car. Both ideas were dumb.

When Arturo got home, Francisco was in their room lying on their bed with headphones on, listening to music. He was wearing his regular clothes, a pair of worn jeans and a white tee shirt.

Arturo told him about Mr. Moreno and the park idea. He didn't tell Francisco that he was the one who had suggested it.

Francisco sneered and laughed.

"Es estúpido," he said. "Don't you know, *hermano,* nobody is going to help us get out of this dump or fix it up?" Then he rolled over on the bed, turning his back on his brother.

Arturo stood quietly in the door for a moment. He felt like an *estúpido niño chico.* Funny, the park had been kind of fun to think about until he told Francisco.

13

CHAPTER 3

"**PARK**?" Papa asked with a frown when Arturo told him of his class's talk about making the neighborhood better. "What is that Anglo teacher putting wild ideas in your head for? What does she know about being poor and nobody? She has a high education and goes home to a nice neighborhood. Park! Nobody cares if you have a place to play or not." Papa reached out and grabbed some *queso fresco* to crumble on his enchilada.

"We were just talking, Papa. It doesn't hurt to talk, does it?" Arturo didn't say that he was the one who had said they needed a place to play.

Mama looked over to Papa to see what he would say.

"Play! When I was your age, I worked until dark every night in a shoe factory in Mexico City. Don't tell me about play. You are a lot better off than I was."

Arturo looked down at his plate, hoping that if he didn't look up Papa would stop sooner. He had heard about the shoe factory and sleeping on the streets so many times.

"Work hard, keep quiet, and don't complain. Remember, you are nobody, and nobody wants to hear what you say." Papa took an emphatic bite of a rolled-up tortilla and chewed it energetically.

"It's just a pretend-like 'what if' game." Arturo tried to sound meek and polite. Miss Fenwick was a nice lady. He didn't like to hear Papa call her ideas wild. He didn't even mention how well Mr. Moreno spoke Spanish. Papa didn't seem to be in the mood to hear it.

"Well, 'what if' a beautiful angel flew down and gave us a lottery ticket for a million dollars?" His father stared at Arturo fiercely. "That's just as smart a question."

Mama looked back and forth between them. She seemed to be disturbed.

After supper Arturo decided not to bother with his dumb assignment. He went across the street to meet Angel at the wheelless hulk of an old, yellow Ford Fairlane station wagon that rested at an angle on some ragged hunks of concrete. Smoke came out of the open window. Angel was there already.

Arturo climbed through the window, carefully avoiding the ragged edge of broken glass. Sitting down on a folded cardboard box, Arturo lit up a cigarette. Angel started talking about how tough and bad his cousin Lobo was. Narrowing his eyes, Angel slowly exhaled a lungful of smoke. "He says he can get me in the *Vatos* in the spring." Angel smiled tauntingly. He knew how badly Arturo wanted to join. "My cousin could get us better shit to smoke than this." Angel smirked devilishly and looked directly into Arturo's eyes. "Francisco could, too."

Arturo scowled. He felt a volcano growing in him. "Hey, man, I better get back. Mama said my aunt and uncle were coming over."

"Don't go. Look, I got some more paint. Want to do some high-class art work?"

"Yeah, sure. Some other time." Arturo started climbing out the window. A ragged edge of glass caught his tee shirt and scratched his back. "See you, man."

Angel was really getting to him lately. He knew more about his brother than Arturo did. Angel knew before he did that Francisco had joined the gang. Now that other stuff!

Sure, Arturo wanted to be one of the *Vatos*. He wanted to dress sharp and drive around in a hot Chevy low rider with his *compañeros*. But dealing drugs? He didn't like the idea — not at all. Huh. Arturo gave a shrug. So what did Angel know, anyway?

On Monday morning in school, Mr. Moreno, looking tall and slim and weirdly bouncy, asked the class to talk about what they would like in their imaginary park. When they had finished, he burst out, saying, "Class, you won't believe this, but after our discussion on Friday, I looked around and found some land for our park!"

Arturo studied Miss Fenwick's face for a clue. Mr. Moreno must mean for their "pretend-like" park. She was smiling as pleasantly as ever. That had to be it.

Juanita, sitting across the aisle, looked puzzled, her dark brows lowered. There were five library books on her desk. Every time Arturo looked at her, she had a bunch of books under her arm or on her desk, or she was reading one. Juanita looked up. "You mean our imaginary park for our assignment?"

"Maybe imaginary, or, who knows? Maybe we could make it real."

"Where?" Clorissa's brown eyes were enormous.

Didn't she know it was just a joke? Arturo rolled his eyes at Angel, who started to laugh. Arturo looked back at Maria, and she laughed too.

"I thought we'd take a walk and look at it." Mr. Moreno leaned against the desk and crossed his arms.

The whole thing was pretty dumb, but if they got out of school, who cared? Arturo yelled, "All right! Let's go!"

Miss Fenwick and Mr. Moreno had everyone line up by

twos in a straight line. Maria wiggled up through the line to stand by Arturo. He turned his head away.

"I'll be your partner, Arturo." Maria twisted a curl of her long hair. There was a teddy bear on her blue tee shirt. Arturo hated that silly picture. He was sick of her always hanging around. She stuck closer to him than his guardian angel.

"Hey, where are we going?" someone yelled.

"You'll see," said Miss Fenwick. "It will be a surprise."

They walked along Elm to Twenty-third. Then they turned left and went past Southwood and Orchard and Bonita. This was the way Arturo went home from school. They passed a bright blue house with white trim. It had a black-iron grille over the windows, and a black-iron fence with points on the top. "That's where Juanita lives," said Clorissa.

"See my pink geraniums?" Juanita's high-pitched voice squeaked. "My friend Ascención gave me cuttings from hers, and I planted them." She beamed proudly.

Most of the houses weren't that nice. Paint was peeling off many of them. One dirty brown house had a big sheet of imitation-brick siding falling off, and the front porch was missing a lot of shingles. A couple of kids, about three or four years old, stood on the porch. They waved across a narrow band of bare dirt.

"That's Angel's house," LeDru yelled, and everyone laughed.

"If people want us to know where they live, let's let them tell us," Miss Fenwick said. She was in the back where a couple of girls were giggling and dragging their feet. Angel was walking ahead of her on tiptoe when he reached up and grabbed LeDru around the throat. LeDru stuck his tongue out and pretended to be choking when Miss Fenwick touched Angel's hands. He turned around in surprise and put his hands innocently by his side.

Clorissa and Trevor were up front with Mr. Moreno, asking questions. That Clorissa, Arturo thought, she looked big enough to be a teacher, walking along in her red sweatshirt and jeans. She seemed smart enough to be a teacher, too.

Arturo heard her telling Mr. Moreno about her friend Vanetta, who was a junior in high school. "She's on the honor roll all the time. Her teachers say she can get a scholarship to a good college." Clorissa seemed to admire Vanetta a lot. Arturo had heard Clorissa talk about her before. She was a runner and got prizes at track meets.

Maria kept talking about a party she was going to, and Arturo tried to ignore her. He began to wonder where they were going. So far it was exactly the way Arturo walked home.

The whole platoon turned a corner and walked down La Luna. At first Arturo felt like yelling, "Hey, are you guys walking me home?" But La Luna suddenly looked awful! So much junk! Paper napkins, plastic forks and spoons, broken bottles, cups, and cardboard boxes turned gray so you couldn't tell what they had come from. Weeds grew up around it all.

As they marched by Julio's *mercado,* the little white wooden market on the corner, several men looked solemnly at the group of children. They didn't smile or speak. Arturo recognized them as drug dealers. They didn't seem to like outsiders coming onto their turf.

Arturo decided not to say that this was his street. He didn't want people to know he lived in such a dump.

Mr. Moreno and Miss Fenwick led the whole class up

La Luna to Arturo and Maria's apartment building. Maria's little sister, who was sitting on the sidewalk, ran up to Maria and grabbed her around the leg. Maria looked embarrassed as she patted her head. Then, with a loud, cheerful voice, Mr. Moreno held up his hand. *"Alto!"* he said. "Stop!"

The whole class stood on the sidewalk in front of Arturo's apartment building. Mr. Moreno pointed across the street at the dump. There were five abandoned cars, along with rusted-out mufflers, smashed cardboard boxes, scraps of lumber, tin cans, a ripped-up sofa the same color as the dirt, and a metal cabinet without any drawers.

Everyone broke ranks, and Angel came over to stand by Arturo. They looked at each other but didn't say a word. Arturo wondered if Angel was thinking of their station-wagon clubhouse, too. He and Angel had investigated every scrap of junk on the lot, but it looked different today. Usually Angel was a loudmouth, but now he was quiet. Arturo felt like someone had come into his room and found his socks and dirty clothes scattered around his unmade bed.

The barbwire-topped metal fence directly behind the dump divided the land from the freeway interchange. Millions of cars roared by every day.

Mr. Moreno pointed exuberantly to the pile of trash backed by concrete and barbed wire. "There's our park!"

The kids were as silent as if they had been hit on the head with a board. They looked bewildered, as though Mr. Moreno had told a bad joke.

Juanita giggled. "It sure doesn't look like a park!" Other kids laughed, too.

Maria looked frightened, then giggled nervously while her little sister clung to her leg. Arturo forced a laugh.

"It doesn't look like a park now," said Miss Fenwick. "Use imagination. Imagination can change things!" Her blue eyes widened as though she really believed it.

Arturo studied her face. She didn't seem to be joking. But what did she know about living on La Luna, a nice lady like her?

"Let's go look at our park." Mr. Moreno glanced left and right, then started across the street. Miss Fenwick reminded everyone to look both ways before following. On the other side, several boys climbed a pile of concrete chunks. LeDru got to the top first and beat his chest. "I'm the king of the mountain." He stood like a young tree on a mountain peak. His long, dark, skinny legs stretched forever below his shorts. LeDru was so skinny that if he swallowed a spoonful of peas, he'd look like a string of beads. His huge tennis shoes were rooted solidly, and he held a large hand out to keep the others off.

That was just like LeDru, always jumping higher, running faster than anyone else, Arturo thought. No wonder! He was so much taller than the other guys. He'd probably be a Harlem Globetrotter when he grew up.

"Come down, LeDru. You could twist your ankle if you caught your foot between those chunks." Miss Fenwick frowned at him, and he walked down.

"Here's something else that can hurt you," said Juanita, holding up a dagger of broken glass. "I saw a little kid playing with some of these yesterday."

Juanita was so sensible, sometimes she sounded more like somebody's mother than a kid. It was kind of weird, but Arturo liked it.

Dust rose in puffs as the kids wandered over the bare, dry ground. Trevor and LeDru were way over by the concrete pillars of the freeway, in the shadows where the gang writing was. LeDru's dark skin and hair blended into the shadows. Trevor's blond hair and white skin stood out like a splash of white paint.

"Come back, boys." Miss Fenwick gestured toward them. "Let's stay together."

"My mother told me not to go under there," Juanita called.

"Let's talk about the lot now that we've seen it," said Mr. Moreno.

Arturo thought he got it. Mr. Moreno wanted them to draw pictures of an imaginary park in the dump and to write about how the park should be—a different kind of class assignment.

"You gotta be joking," Angel said, finally finding his tongue. "This is just a dump."

"It doesn't have to stay a dump," Miss Fenwick answered calmly.

Arturo was puzzled again. Were they both crazy like Papa said? Everyone was silent as though totally confused.

Clorissa crossed her arms and looked down at the ground. She stood almost as tall as Miss Fenwick and quite a bit wider. "No one would make that dump into a park for us."

"Don't say that, Clorissa. How can we say something can't be done if it hasn't even been tried?"

Miss Fenwick always said things like that.

Standing beside Clorissa, Juanita looked even tinier. She was wearing a white puffed-sleeve blouse under her blue bib overalls. "That would take a lot of money, and what do we know about getting parks made? We are just kids," Juanita said.

"Yeah, we're just kids!" echoed several voices.

"Maybe some people who know how to do it would help us." Mr. Moreno didn't sound discouraged. "Who might help us? Who makes parks?"

There was a long silence. Then Angel said, "Nobody in our barrio, that's for sure."

When everyone stopped laughing, Miss Fenwick said, "How about the government? Maybe the city would help us."

A lot of kids yelled, "No way!" "Forget it!" "Nah!" Even Arturo found himself speaking up. "The government doesn't care about us. My father says—"

"Yeah, well, this is a pretty dumpy neighborhood all right." Trevor licked his lips eagerly, then burst out. "I don't blame them for not caring about it. Nobody cares about it! If we were up in Washington State where I'm from, where it's green and there are a lot of trees and things—" He stopped suddenly and put his hand over his mouth.

Arturo stared at Trevor coldly. Everyone else glared, too.

"Let's not decide what is possible before we try." Miss Fenwick looked so certain. "Let's play 'what if' and let our imaginations loose. Let's pretend it's possible and make designs in art class."

"We can compose a letter to the Los Angeles Department of Recreation and Parks. Maybe they will make a minipark for us." Mr. Moreno slapped his hands together eagerly. "It doesn't hurt to ask."

Miss Fenwick looked at him. "It will also help us learn something about how our government works."

"I don't know. My mother says when you are just a little bug, stay out of the way or you might be stepped on," Maria muttered to Arturo as they walked back to school.

CHAPTER 4

WHEN ARTURO GOT HOME FROM SCHOOL,
he grabbed a banana, a glass of milk, and a tortilla. Sitting down at the kitchen table, he opened his tablet and took out a pencil. So it was just a stupid game. What of it? He drew a curving line the width of the paper, then another about an inch apart from it. There! A walk through the park. Now it needed some orange and yellow flowers along the edge. Arturo peeled his banana eagerly, took a bite, then drew two benches. This was a good game. Wouldn't it be great if it were for real?

No one was home yet. Francisco was hardly ever home anymore. Sometimes he didn't even come home for supper. That made Mama worried and Papa mad.

Why not have a sand box, a round one, in the park? The Lopez kids could play there instead of on the stairs. Arturo drew a nice, smooth, concrete edge around the sand box to divide it from the grass. Yes, grass! Arturo made a big circle with a sweep of his pencil. While he scratched little short lines for grass, he remembered trees. How could he forget? There was so much hot concrete around his apartment building and asphalt around the school yard. He'd have trees in his park. He drew a big, puffy shape for a tree and put down a couple of straight lines for a trunk right over the grass. As he did, he heard the sound of footsteps on the stairs, then Papa coming in. Arturo took the last bite of his banana and put down the peel. *"Buenas tardes,* Papa."

His father took off his hard hat and Day-Glo orange

vest, which helped drivers see him while he worked on the highways, and put them on the kitchen counter with his lunch box.

Arturo continued drawing a little building in the park.

"Is that homework, *mijo?*" Papa looked over Arturo's shoulder. "Just because I can't read letters doesn't mean I can't tell that drawing is just playing, not learning."

Quickly Arturo folded up the tablet. "It's kind of a game, Papa, but it's homework, too."

"That fairy tale about a park, hah? Don't pay attention to that Anglo woman. In a couple more years maybe you can get a job in the auto-body shop that hired Francisco."

Is that what Francisco had told them? Papa thought that Francisco worked in an auto-body shop? Arturo's eyes grew wide. He thought of how his brother must have lied. But he didn't know for sure. Maybe Francisco really did have a job at an auto-body shop. He wasn't going to ask.

"It sure is just a game," Papa continued. "Baseball and soccer are better games than that. At least there are winners in those games." His father walked into the bathroom to wash his hands. "Learn some figuring. You need that in an auto-body shop, or upholstery shop, or wherever you work."

Arturo put away the tablet. Papa was probably right; a real game was better. He put his Dodgers cap on backward and grabbed his hard rubber ball with markings on it to make it look like a baseball. Maybe Angel would like to play some catch. He'd try to forget how Angel had been bugging him.

Arturo found Angel at Julio's market with some tough-looking dudes. "Hey, Angel, come on. Let's play catch."

Angel threw his cigarette onto the sidewalk, stepped on it, and followed Arturo.

They tossed the ball back and forth along the street. Angel jumped into the street to catch a throw from Arturo, then tossed it back to him. He could throw pretty good for such a little guy. They started throwing it farther and farther. Arturo backed up fast on the sidewalk as he saw a high one coming. He missed. The ball came down on the hood of Mr. Lopez's old blue Pontiac. Arturo heard the metal go *sproing!* The worst thing was that Mr. Lopez was right there, wiping off the dashboard. He jumped out and yelled, "You kids stop throwing that ball! If you dent my car, your butts are going to be in a sling!" Mr. Lopez had fire in his eye. "Arturo! You hear me?"

Arturo picked up the ball as it rolled into the street and gave it an easy toss to Angel. "Okay, Mr. Lopez, we'll leave. Sorry, *perdón!*"

They tossed the ball back and forth over La Luna but almost hit a car going by, and the driver shook his fist. Then Maria's little sister ran after a ball that went into the street, and Arturo had to catch her while a car swerved to keep from hitting her.

Finally the boys sat down on the curb, discouraged. Then Arturo said, "Hey, come on," and Angel followed him into the apartment house, up past the third floor, and onto the roof.

The roof was almost flat with a slight slope and a short wall around the edge. Arturo backed away from Angel to the other side of the roof, then tossed an easy one, just warming up. Angel tossed a harder one back to him. The roof creaked as Arturo ran. The ball slammed right into his palm, and he shot the ball back. Angel threw a fast one, and Arturo trotted off after it, clumping over the pebbly asphalt roofing. He ran. He reached. The ball catapulted beyond the roof's edge.

In anger Arturo pounded his palm with his other fist and glanced over the roof to see the ball dropping into the street by Mr. Lopez's car again. Arturo hit his forehead and made a face.

"You missed it, you get it," yelled Angel, swinging his arms loosely as though he were pitching. Arturo climbed down and found the ball under the rear of Mr. Lopez's car. He had to crawl on his belly to reach it.

"I thought I told you kids to stop playing ball!" Mr. Lopez said, glaring.

Angel leaned over the roof and yelled, "Hey, man, did you go out to buy another ball or something?"

Arturo stood up and brushed the dirt off his knees. By the time he got back up on the roof, Angel was frowning.

"Come on, Speedy, play ball!" he yelled.

They got in a number of good, solid exchanges. Then Angel threw a hard, fast one directly at Arturo. The throw was high, so Arturo backed up quickly with his arm in the air. He couldn't miss it after muffing that other one. Angel hadn't missed a one. With his eye locked on the ball, he took a couple more running steps and reached for it as it veered toward the edge.

"Hey, look out!" Angel yelled.

The ball touched Arturo's fingertips. He closed his hand tightly around it. Then his leg hit the wall at the roof's edge. His knees buckled, and he started to fall backward over the edge. Dropping the ball quickly, he grabbed the wall so hard his fingers hurt. Then he stood up carefully. He stood quietly, his head down and his feet apart. Angel ran up and grabbed Arturo's arm.

"Hey, *compa*, you almost went over!"

Arturo breathed deeply. "But I didn't, and I caught it! You saw me catch it!" Arturo's heart was still racing.

Then Arturo saw Mr. Garcia, Maria's father, standing on the sidewalk looking up. "You crazy kids get down from there. I can't hear my TV with all that galloping. You'll break the roof. If you don't break your necks, the landlord will do it for you."

"Yeah, man," said Angel. "Arturo was about to go down anyway." Angel laughed wildly and punched Arturo's arm.

The next day, everyone got going on the park assignment. After writing a letter to the Department of Recreation and Parks, the class focused on visualizing the minipark. Juanita tore a piece of newsprint off a big roll of paper. "I think this is neat, Miss Fenwick, designing a park. Do you think the city might really make that lot into a park?"

"Let's do what we can and see what happens." Miss Fenwick was wearing a little pale pink lipstick, but she had on a baggy gray sweater big enough for an elephant.

Maria drew a tree with a green crayon, then made pink flowers all around it. Clorissa drew swings on green grass, and Trevor made a big, blue patch in the middle of his paper for a pond with some ducks swimming on it. He said his drawing reminded him of Washington State.

But Arturo drew the whole park, starting with what he had done at home. He was surprised that he could see it all in his mind just as if he were flying over it in an airplane. The park was shaped like a piece of pie filled with trees and bushes and flowers. His park even had a slide, swings, and traveling bars. His own world came flowing out of his pencil and onto the paper. He finished it by drawing two little buildings with signs on them: one sign said BOYS and one sign said GIRLS.

Maria looked at the picture and giggled. Juanita came over to look at his drawing. She slid and whirled around to Miss Fenwick. "Look at what Arturo did! He's doing the whole park."

LeDru looked at Arturo's design. "Hey, man, I don't see any place to play basketball." Then someone else yelled, "How about picnic benches and drinking fountains?"

Arturo was carefully drawing stones in a wall by the freeway. He put his hands over his ears. "I can't put in everything. There isn't room!"

The drawing started everyone talking about what Arturo should and shouldn't put in. But Angel sat in the back of the room working on his picture.

"Is that for the park, Angel?" Clorissa pointed at Angel's drawing of a purple low rider with orange flames on the hood.

"What would you like in our park, Angel?" Miss Fenwick smoothed her skirt and sat down beside him.

"There won't be any park," Angel said. "I'm drawing a car like I am going to get someday." Angel put down the purple crayon and picked up a black one to color a tire.

The whole class fell silent as though waiting. Juanita wound a strand of her long, dark brown hair around her finger. "You are so negative, Angel! How can you do anything that way?"

Arturo smiled at her. Juanita might be a book owl with those round glasses, but she had big, strong ideas.

"How long do you think it'll be before we hear from the Recreation Department?" Clorissa asked while sharpening her pencil.

28

Miss Fenwick looked up from examining Arturo's drawing and smiled mischievously. "It will take a couple of weeks, I'm sure, once they get our letter. If it takes much longer than that, maybe we'll have to call them."

"Call them?" Juanita's eyes enlarged eagerly behind her glasses. "You mean, like one of us?"

"Of course!" said Miss Fenwick. "How about you, Arturo?" But Arturo made such a terrified face that Miss Fenwick said, "All right, you don't seem quite ready. How about you, Juanita?"

Juanita's face turned as red as a chili pepper. She started to giggle and covered her face. Arturo knew how she felt. Breathing deeply, he relaxed completely. Talking to important grown-up people was scary.

One week later when Mr. Moreno came to class, they still hadn't heard from the city. "Governments never seem to respond quickly," he said. "We'll give them a little longer before we call."

But after another week, everyone decided it was time to call. The whole class walked down to the office to listen while Juanita made the call.

She spoke stiffly, as if she were reading from a book.

"Hello, my name is Juanita Rivera. I am calling for Miss Fenwick's sixth-grade class at Southwood Elementary School. We wrote a letter about . . ." Then she stopped while they transferred her to someone else. She repeated the same words again, and they transferred her again. By the third time, she was pretty good at saying the words. In her normal voice, she told the person on the phone what they wanted to know. When she hung up the phone, she had a proud smile. "I never thought I could do that." Her voice was a whisper.

Then she said to all her listeners, "They said they were about ready to answer our letter." She jumped up and down, exclaiming, "I did it! I did it!"

The following Monday Miss Fenwick brought a letter to the class from the Recreation and Parks Department. Mr. Moreno was there, too. Miss Fenwick tore open the letter and read:

Dear Miss Fenwick, Mr. Moreno, and boys and girls:

Thank you for your letter and the suggestion that the city make a minipark for your neighborhood out of the parcel of land near Marina Freeway on La Luna. We appreciate your interest in our city and your suggestion for improving it. Unfortunately, due to cuts in the budget for the department and the necessity to make repairs on many of the existing parks in our city, we will not be able to consider developing and maintaining new park property, even one this small. We are sorry we can't be of more help. Thank you for your interest in improving our city.

The whole class let out enormous groans and sighs even before Miss Fenwick had finished reading.

Maria poked Arturo and whispered, "My father said the government wouldn't do anything."

"I told you it wouldn't be any use." Angel jumped up from his desk and held his hand up high. "Now do you believe me?"

Some of the faces turning toward Angel were angry; some were disappointed. Juanita frowned. Clorissa said sadly, "I didn't want to believe you, but maybe I have to."

30

"What about you, Arturo?" Mr. Moreno held Arturo's park plan up. There it was, thought Arturo, a clean, pretty place that had come out of his mind but would never become real. The class waited for his answer. "Do you think it isn't any use trying?"

"I don't know." Arturo's voice was weak. He knew it was a game. Why was he unhappy? "I don't want to give up, but it's probably not going to happen. Why should anyone give us a park?"

There was a chorus of groans as if Arturo had punched them all in the stomach. Even Mr. Moreno wasn't as cheerful as usual. "Let's think about it overnight. Tomorrow we can decide if there is something else we can do. Or," he paused, letting them consider the idea seriously, "maybe we will want to give up. That will be your decision."

While he was walking home from school, Arturo wondered why he was unhappy. Hadn't his father and Francisco told him not to expect any help? But Arturo still wanted their idea to work. He wanted it so bad.

"Arturo!"

Arturo turned to see his brother getting out of a car. He could see two other guys in the car before it drove off. They were *Vatos* and several years older than Francisco. Everybody knew they were dealers. Arturo's heart felt heavy; maybe Angel was right. Francisco strode toward Arturo, looking *muy guapo*, very handsome. He wore a gold earring with a little cross hanging from it and a gold chain around his neck over a new shirt.

"Hey, little brother, here's something for you." He ruffled Arturo's hair and handed him a plastic bag with BUY-RITE printed on it. Arturo pulled out a brand new camouflage-print tee shirt. It looked like a guerrilla fighter's.

Talk about sharp! Maybe the *Vatos* would let him join before they let Angel. Suddenly he felt six-feet tall.

"*Gracias*, Francisco. Thanks a lot!" Arturo punched his brother on the upper arm. "You are one cool dude."

Yeah, Arturo thought, his big brother knew what was what.

CHAPTER 5

"YOU FORGOT YOUR LUNCH, MARIA," Mrs. Garcia called out the window as Maria trotted down the apartment stairs behind Arturo. Wearing his new camouflage-print tee shirt, he felt very grown up and confident.

"Okay, Mama. Hey, wait for me, Arturo," she yelled while she scampered upstairs.

Arturo sighed with annoyance but stood waiting and holding the heavy door. Maria was back in a second, jumping down three steps at a time with her lunch sack in her hand.

"Come right home after school, Maria. I want you to take care of Consuelo while I go shopping."

"Okay, Mama." Maria trotted to catch up with Arturo. Boy, she sure was pink this morning, he thought. She wore a pink tee shirt with a big flower on it and matching pink shorts. She even had a ruffly pink hair ribbon around a puff of dark curls that stuck up on one side of her head. Tiny, sparkly earrings twinkled in her pierced ears when she smiled at Arturo.

He stared at her. She was always sticking to him like chewing gum, but it was getting worse. Look at all her fancy stuff! He'd never noticed she had earrings.

"I like your shirt, Arturo. Is it new?"

Standing a little straighter and half closing his eyes, he said, "Yeah, Francisco got it for me a few days ago."

They walked along silently past an old Pontiac Firebird missing both doors. "There's Mr. Moreno's park," Maria said, giggling. "My parents say he's a dreamer, and dreamers should wake up."

Sometimes Arturo thought the same thing, but he didn't like to hear Maria say it. Something stubborn in him asked, Why couldn't they have a park if they wanted one? That wouldn't sound cool though, so he said, "Hey, we better hurry," and started to run.

"Wait for me," Maria called and began running after him.

What a pest, Arturo thought. Why hadn't he left for school without her?

Even before Mr. Moreno got to class that morning, Miss Fenwick and the kids began talking about the park. Angel spoke first. "It's loco. Nobody's going to give us a park."

"Why shouldn't we have a park?" asked Juanita. "We hardly have any place to play."

"Maybe if we asked higher up in the government." Trevor was leaning on his arms and looking up through the long blond hair falling across his eyes. "My father teaches political science at USC, and he says—"

"What do you think, Miss Fenwick?" Clorissa rubbed her hands together impatiently. "Don't you think if we all worked together that we could get the park going?"

"Why not try?" Miss Fenwick smiled encouragingly. "Harder things have been done. Even if the dump doesn't become a park, we would all learn a lot."

As soon as Mr. Moreno stepped in the door, Clorissa spoke up loudly and clearly. "I want to keep trying, Mr. Moreno."

Arturo glanced at his design for the park hanging on the bulletin board and burst out with, "What can we lose?" Then his hand flew to his mouth in surprise at what he had said.

Maria and Angel looked at him like he was loco.

"Trevor said we could go to the higher-ups in the government," Juanita piped up. "Who would that be?"

"Who is at the very top of our city government?" Mr. Moreno was playing with a pencil and grinning. He knew already.

"The mayor!" said Trevor.

"Mayor Broderick!" LeDru added, waving his arm wildly.

"What would be the best way to approach him?"

Miss Fenwick was going to suggest writing another letter, thought Arturo with an inward groan.

"What would influence him?" Mr. Moreno asked.

"If he knew a lot of people who might vote for him next time wanted the park." Arturo felt his face get hot with embarrassment as soon as the words popped out. Why did he care anyhow?

"Yeah, Arturo," yelled LeDru.

"What a wonderful idea, Arturo," said Miss Fenwick. "And how do we let him know that?"

Juanita was bouncing up and down in her seat and waving her hand wildly. "With a petition!"

"That's a grrrrrrreat idea, Juanita." Mr. Moreno punched his palm with his fist. "Let's do it!"

"What's a petition?" LeDru looked puzzled.

Everybody was quiet as if maybe others didn't know either. Arturo was glad LeDru had asked because he didn't know much about petitions.

"This is a good opportunity for a real-life lesson, students," Miss Fenwick said, getting out the social-science textbook. "For tomorrow's discussion I want you to read pages ten through eighteen. This section tells what processes are available to citizens in a democratic society for making changes in that society. Some of these methods are initiative, referendum, and recall. Since Mr. Moreno is majoring in political science, he can tell us about petitions now."

Mr. Moreno seemed eager to talk. "Citizens in a democracy have a lot of power," he started. But at the word "power," Angel loudly said, "Ha! Ha! Ha!" Those laughs sounded like three insulting slaps.

Mr. Moreno pointed a finger at him and continued, "Yes, they do, Angel, but many people do not use it—don't even vote." Then he told them how petitions can be used by people to influence individuals or organizations to do or not to do certain things. A petition is a written request, he told them, signed by people who agree on what the petition is asking for. The signed petition is then presented to the individual or department, asking for a response.

"So let's send a petition to Mayor Broderick." Clorissa sounded as if she were already on the city council.

"Maybe in art class we can print signs to carry around with our petition." Juanita waved her hand and talked at the same time.

"Absolutely!" Miss Fenwick seemed excited. "Now let's write our petition." Taking a piece of chalk, she wrote, "Dear Mayor Broderick," then stopped. "Okay, girls and boys. What will get the mayor on our side?"

She and Mr. Moreno asked everyone for suggestions and wrote them down on the board. When she asked Angel what to put in, he waved his hand at her. "Naaah! The mayor won't pay any attention."

Kids started yelling at him then. "Shut up, Angel!" LeDru said. "It don't hurt to try."

Mr. Moreno had done some research on the neighborhood, so he added a few sentences, too. The finished letter said:

Dear Mayor Broderick,

We are sixth graders in Miss Fenwick and Mr. Moreno's class in Southwood Elementary School. Mr. Moreno is Miss Fenwick's student teacher. We are writing to ask your help in making a minipark in our neighborhood. Our school is very crowded, so there are always a lot of students who need a place to play. We play in the street or on rooftops sometimes. We don't even have a blade of grass in our schoolyard. It is dangerous to play in busy streets, but kids want to play so badly that they do it anyway. Mr. Moreno says also that our neighborhood is one of the highest crime areas in the city, and that we really need a park.

With our teachers we found a piece of land near the Marina Freeway on-ramp. It is about twelve thousand square feet and would make a nice minipark, but it is too small for anything else. Please do what you can to help us. We have collected signatures and addresses of grown-ups who also want us to have this park, and we are sending them with this letter.

We hope to hear from you soon.

Respectfully,

Miss Fenwick and Mr. Moreno's class
Southwood Elementary School

"I think we should all sign it," said LeDru.

"I couldn't agree more," responded Mr. Moreno.

Arturo felt a smile growing on his face. He couldn't stop smiling. Maybe Francisco and Mama and Papa were right about the city not paying attention to them, but the petition sounded so good and important! It didn't hurt to try. He turned around to look at Angel, who was staring up at the front of the class as if he had been surprised. Usually he looked so cool with his eyes half closed. Now his wide-open eyes made him look like a kid who believed in the Easter Bunny.

Juanita said that she would copy the letter, so Miss Fenwick gave her some good paper. During art class everyone made posters. Arturo made a poster with a picture of a slide. He printed "WE WANT A PARK" in big, block letters with a broad marking pen. Then he made some signs in Spanish. Maria drew two children with blue and yellow flowers on her poster. She asked Arturo to do the printing. He picked up a red marking pen and wrote, *"¡Necesitamos un parque!"*

"You're a good printer." Maria smiled.

Arturo's face grew hot. He thought about the letters he had sprayed on his apartment-building foundation by the trash bins.

"Yeah, I've had practice."

While everyone finished the posters, Mr. Moreno made copies of the petition. "Here, class," he said, handing them out. "There's a lot of work for us. Take these home and get as many grown-ups as you can to sign."

"This afternoon I'll try to get permission for us to gather signatures in the shopping center." Miss Fenwick waved at everyone as they left. "Get lots of names!"

"I'm going to get gazillions of names," Clorissa said. She strode out confidently with a stack of petitions.

Arturo picked up three sheets and ran out, eager to get started. Angel yelled at him, "You're wasting your time!"

What are you doing that's so important? Arturo thought as he walked right by Angel without a word, strutting like Francisco.

CHAPTER
6

"ARTURO? Are you in there?" Mama knocked on Arturo's bedroom door.

"Yes, Mama."

"Are you all right?"

"I'm fine. I'm just studying."

Mama was quiet for a minute as if she couldn't believe it. "Studying?"

After dinner that Friday evening, Arturo had gone into his bedroom and pulled the blankets up on his unmade bed. He sat down and picked up his book, *People and Government*, hidden under his sweater on the bed. He wanted to know more about petitions. He didn't believe that the mayor would pay any attention to them, but Miss Fenwick said it didn't hurt to try.

Mama opened the door. She had her apron on. "So, you are doing your studies? Come out where the light is better."

"I'm all right here, Mama."

"No, come out. You will ruin your eyes in that light."

He couldn't read out there where Papa asked questions and made fun of him.

"It's better here, Mama. It's quieter."

Now Papa looked through the open door. "What's the matter, *mijo?*" Papa asked.

"I'm studying, Papa."

"What are you studying?"

Arturo rolled over with annoyance. He looked up,

frowning. "I'm reading about petitions, Papa. My class is making a petition to ask Mayor Broderick for a minipark across the street by the freeway." Arturo didn't mention the petitions he had brought home. Papa would be angry because he didn't know how to read or write and couldn't sign his name.

"Petitions! Is your teacher still talking about that park! That teacher is as crazy as a dollar watch." Papa left and slammed the door shut. Arturo didn't feel like reading anymore.

The whole idea did seem dumb. Good things like a park didn't happen in this neighborhood. Arturo got up and combed his hair carefully in the mirror. He squinted at his upper lip and ran his finger over it. He sighed. Nothing there yet. If he went out, maybe he'd see some of the guys. Maybe he'd even see Francisco. He shouldn't have gotten angry with Angel.

He hardly ever saw Francisco any more, because Francisco slept late and was gone most of the night. Mama asked Arturo if he had been to the shop where Francisco worked. When Arturo said no, she said, "I am so worried. Francisco is hardly ever at home."

"I know, Mama," Arturo said. "He's probably with his friends." That wasn't a lie, but Arturo felt uncomfortable. He was afraid that Francisco wasn't pounding out fenders. "I think I'll go out and find someone to play stickball, Mama. I'll be back soon." As Arturo started to walk out, he thought of the petition and went back into his room to get it. It couldn't hurt to try, could it?

The October evening was warm and pleasant. He walked down La Luna to Julio's *mercado* on the corner. Arturo couldn't see inside because the building had only a narrow strip of iron-barred windows above head level. He could hear talking and laughing. Since it was Friday night, a lot of men were standing around drinking beer. Arturo went in.

Mr. Ochoa was arguing with Julio about something and waving his can of beer for emphasis. Then he took a long drink and wiped off his bushy moustache. He looked thirsty. He had dust all over his clothes and heavy work boots from his job at an excavation site.

"Would you sign a petition, Mr. Ochoa, to help get a minipark for the children in our neighborhood?"

"Do what?" asked Mr. Ochoa.

Arturo glanced to the side at a teenager standing silent and unsmiling near the beer cooler. He had a long, angular face with a tear tattooed by the inner corner of his eye, and he wore a black tee shirt with torn-out sleeves. Arturo didn't know him.

"This is a petition to Mayor Broderick asking him to make a park on that dump on La Luna," Arturo explained. "Would you help us by signing it?" Arturo wondered who the guy by the cooler was. He looked like bad news from the Thirty-thirders, but what was he doing over here in *Vatos* territory?

Three more men gathered around Arturo. A couple of them wore blue work shirts, and one young man was all slicked up in a long-sleeved white shirt tucked into his sharply pressed gray slacks. Probably getting ready to pick up his girl for a night on the town, Arturo thought. The young man laughed and said, "What good will it do?" But the other two men signed. A fourth man said, "I'll sign it. My kids are four and five and could use some grass and a swing to play on." He reached for the pen Arturo handed him. Hearing him, a thin, gray-haired man lounging by the

41

door said, "All right, what does it hurt to sign?" and two more men signed.

"What's the use? No one will pay any attention," the young man with the tattooed tear said. One of the workmen yelled out, "Just admit that you can't sign your name." Everyone laughed, but the guy with the tattoo turned and left quickly.

All weekend Arturo carried the petition around and got people to sign. He met Mrs. Lopez as she walked, pushing the baby in its stroller. When he told her about the park, she said she wanted some petitions to take to her friends at church. Aunt Yolanda and Uncle Juan came over to leave their baby with Mama while they went to Uncle Juan's cousin's wedding in El Monte. They signed the petition, but Aunt Yolanda said, "I'll do it for you, Arturo, but don't get your hopes up."

Papa looked on silently while they were signing.

On Monday morning Arturo took to school two pages full of signatures and another with fourteen names, which he had gathered over the weekend. He felt so good. Almost everyone had some names—if only those of their own families. Too bad the Lopez kids were too little to sign, he thought. Maria put her petition with five names on it on the stack.

Miss Fenwick did not look very happy this morning. "I talked to the activity advisor about us taking a field trip to the shopping center with our signs and petitions, but she told me it was a crazy idea." She looked discouraged for a moment but then lifted her head up high and smiled her usual pretty smile. "Then I talked to the principal, and she said, 'Go ahead. It's good to have the kids learn how things are done!' "

"Hurrah!" A spontaneous shout arose. Trevor clapped his

cupped hands to make a loud sound, and LeDru jumped high enough to make a basket.

Trevor had brought sticks from home, and they stapled their posters onto them. That afternoon they walked to the shopping center, carrying their posters. "WE NEED A PARK!" "HELP US BUILD A PARK!" *"¡NECESITAMOS UN PARQUE!"* *"¡AYÚDANOS A CONSTRUIR UN PARQUE!"* The signs had bright-colored pictures of trees, flowers, swings, wading pools, and children. Arturo lifted his sign a little higher. He felt he was doing something important.

The class gathered outside the market. As people went in and out, the kids asked them to sign their petition. One lady with a ten-pound sack of *masa harina* loaded into her baby's stroller signed.

Arturo went with some of the kids into the parking lot to speak to people. "Would you please sign a petition to help us get a park?" Arturo asked. He was getting better at asking.

"Oh, I hope you get your park!" one plump woman said. "Maybe my baby can play there when she's big enough to play outside."

Then Arturo approached a man wearing a navy blue sailing cap. A few gray hairs stuck out from under it, and he had a scraggly white beard on his bright pink face. When Arturo asked him to sign, he said, "I can't read that Spanish sign, son."

"I'll translate it for you," Arturo said, but the man waved his hand and walked off. When Arturo glanced at Miss Fenwick, she said, "That's his privilege, Arturo."

LeDru stood next to a city bus stopped to pick up passengers. With one step of his long legs, he got onto the bus and, after asking a couple questions, the driver signed.

Angel bought a grape popsicle and stood against a lamp-post, eating it and looking bored. After he finished the popsicle, he threw the wrapper and stick on the asphalt and put his hands into his pockets.

"You pick that up, Angel," Juanita snapped at him and pointed at the trash.

"Pick it up yourself!" he yelled.

"Mr. Moreno, Angel shouldn't throw trash around, should he? Especially when we are all trying to improve our neighborhood?" Arturo stood smiling at her. She was so little but could be so fierce. When she believed in things, she wasn't afraid to say so—even if people didn't like what she said.

"What do you think, class? Should we throw trash on the ground?"

Angel was slouching by the lamppost, frowning sulkily. He looked sideways from under the curls hanging over his forehead.

"No!" everyone yelled. Trevor and LeDru walked over and stood by Angel. Arturo stood in front of him, and they all stared at him.

"Oh, all right." He reached down, wadded up the wrapper, and tossed it into a trash bin.

Angel didn't ask anyone to sign petitions. He didn't even carry any petitions. Arturo tried to ignore him because he knew Angel wanted to be noticed being annoying.

Most of the people they met were women, and they usually signed. "Pardon me, ma'am," Clorissa would say. "Would you like to help us children of Southwood Elementary School build a minipark in our neighborhood?" Clorissa got lots of names because people paid attention to her clear, strong voice.

Arturo could see that Juanita was shy about talking to people. She was so tiny that people stared at her as if she were a stray kitten. But quite a few signed, and she got better at asking.

Even Maria got some names. Everybody was doing pretty well. As they filled the sheets, they handed them to Mr. Moreno or Miss Fenwick. Arturo filled three sheets.

Pretty soon Miss Fenwick said, "Time to leave, kids. You don't want to miss your buses."

Just then, three tough-looking homeboy-types came out of the market. Arturo didn't recognize them. Could they be Thirty-thirders? He decided to stay out of their way. Angel, on his way into the market, ran into one of them, and it looked to Arturo like Angel spoke to him. He had slicked-back hair with a little pigtail hanging down and a dangling hoop earring. Then the dude strode over and smirked at Arturo. "Hey, *niño,* what you doing?"

Arturo started to walk away. The guy was head and shoulders taller than he was, and Arturo could practically feel the dude's hands on him. The other kids had followed Miss Fenwick off the lot, except for Juanita, who was trailing behind.

"Hey, *niño,* I'm talking to you. What you doing?" The guy grabbed the front of Arturo's tee shirt. His two friends were grinning.

Arturo felt panicky. Sweat burst out all over his body. Should he yell for help? "W—W—Would you like to sign our petition to get a park on La Luna?" Arturo decided to play it straight. "We need a place to—"

"Let's see your petition," he said, and he ripped the sheets from Arturo's hands. Then, with a hard jab to the stomach, he knocked the wind out of Arturo and sent him reeling backward. Losing his balance, Arturo fell to the asphalt. One of the guy's friends grabbed Arturo's sign, tore it in two, broke the stick, and strutted off.

The first guy looked down at Arturo and said, "Oh, sorry, here's your petition." He tore it into pieces and threw them over Arturo where he lay on the asphalt, doubled up with pain.

As the other two walked off quickly, Juanita looked around the corner of the market. "Arturo, come on. . . . Oh, what happened?" She ran toward him, yelling, "Mr. Moreno, come quick!"

As Arturo painfully got to his feet, he saw a car move away from the curb, carrying the three guys. It looked like the guy with the tattooed tear from Julio's was driving. For sure they were Thirty-thirders, Arturo thought. They had to be. Mr. Moreno came rushing over to Arturo, who straightened up slowly while Angel smirked at him.

"What happened?" asked Mr. Moreno. "Are you all right?"

"I'm . . . all . . . right. Some creep hit me in the stomach." As he struggled to get his wind back, the class gathered around him, asking questions.

Arturo looked over at Angel. He knew that Angel had told the guy to attack him. He'd love to beat the crud out of the little creep. He grabbed Angel by the front of his tee shirt, but Mr. Moreno grabbed Arturo's shoulder. "Let's settle this later, Arturo."

Mr. Moreno stooped over and picked up the scraps of petition. "What we have here is a jigsaw puzzle for someone to put together. In a democracy, differences of opinion are within our rights, but punching someone in the stomach is definitely not within those rights." As he walked along with a hand on his stomach, Arturo glanced over at Angel, who had retreated a safe distance into the group. If those guys were Thirty-thirders, what business did Angel have telling them to hit him, and what were they doing in the *Vatos* territory?

CHAPTER 7

MISS FENWICK hadn't seen the incident and was hurrying people to get in line and back to the school. "We can count the names tomorrow," she said.

"Ohhh, no," came the disappointed cry.

But on the walk back to school, Trevor said, "How many names do you have, Maria?"

"Eleven."

"Okay, added to mine that makes twenty-two and . . ." Pretty soon thirty-five kids in the class were adding their names together.

"I've got fourteen."

"I've got eighteen."

Everyone talked and joked. Arturo had twenty-eight names, and knowing that made him feel a little better. His stomach was almost back to normal. He wasn't going to forget those thugs, though—or that little punk Angel.

"Boy, one lady was really rude. She said, 'Don't bother me, little girl,'" said Juanita. "But then another one said, 'Bless you, dear. I hope Mayor Broderick listens to you.' I guess there are some nice people and some cranky ones."

"I got forty-three names." Clorissa waved her petitions and handed them to Miss Fenwick.

"Wow! That makes 183." Trevor's voice rose above the others.

"I didn't get any names. I got something better—a popsicle!" said Angel. Arturo walked right up to him and grabbed him around the arms. He could have pulverized the little jerk right there. But instead he just glared at him, squeezed his arms hard, and pushed him away—hard! Angel looked frightened.

What a mouthy little coward, Arturo thought, and he shook his fist at Angel. "You're lucky I didn't give you a knuckle sandwich."

"Angel, you have the wrong name." Juanita's tiny voice was bold. "You should be called *Diablo.*"

Everyone laughed at the thought of Angel being called Devil.

"Three hundred and fifty-seven names, counting the ones we already have at school." Trevor waved the sheets of paper victoriously over his head before handing them to Mr. Moreno.

"Yea! Yea!" everyone shouted.

Miss Fenwick could hardly be heard above the cheering. "I'll mail the petition to Mayor Broderick tonight. You kids have done wonderful work, no matter what happens."

"You told us that before," yelled LeDru.

"We want a wonderful park for our wonderful work," Clorissa shouted. There was a big cheer. This might just be a game, but the game was getting exciting, and Arturo wanted his team to win.

As Arturo started to school the next morning, Mrs. Lopez stepped into the hall from her apartment and called, "Arturo!"

When he saw her with a loose, blue-striped top on, Arturo wondered if there was another little Lopez on the way.

She reached her hand into a pocket shaped like a gigantic strawberry, pulled out some folded papers, and handed them to him.

While he was opening them, the youngest Lopez—Dolores—toddled to the door wearing pajamas with a duck on the front. Teetering up, she smiled broadly, displaying her tiny front teeth. She held out a slobbery cookie to him to share. He rubbed her dark curls but politely refused the cookie.

"Take those to your teacher." Mrs. Lopez handed him some petitions. "Some of my friends from church have signed them. *Buena suerte.*" She picked up Dolores, who was waving bye-bye.

"*Gracias,* señora," Arturo waved the petitions and started down the stairs. She had actually wished him luck. It was the first time anyone in the building had said anything about the park project other than to say that he and his class were loco.

Miss Fenwick had hardly walked in the door before Trevor spoke up. "How long do you think it will take to hear from the mayor?" Arturo thought that Miss Fenwick was looking very fresh and perky in a flowered blouse and white pants. She laughed. "Let's give the man a few days to get it and read it. We can't do anything more about the letter, so let's concentrate on something we can do. How about making a scale model from Arturo's plan?"

Arturo got a feeling of importance again. It was great. He could hardly wait for the mayor to answer them. But Miss Fenwick was right: It would take awhile to hear from the mayor; they should get busy on something else.

"A scale model?" said LeDru. "I've made scale-model planes."

"What is a scale model, class?" Miss Fenwick asked.

"Something real little," said Juanita.

"A scale model doesn't have to be little. You can have

scale models that are bigger than the original," Trevor said, raising his hand. "Scale means that for every foot or inch of a thing, the model has a certain number of feet or inches, see?"

Juanita wrinkled her nose in confusion, but Clorissa spoke up calmly. "Maybe we should talk about ratio, Miss Fenwick."

"Wonderful, Clorissa. You have obviously read your math book." Miss Fenwick pointed at Clorissa with approval.

For arithmetic that day they studied ratio and how many inches or fractions of an inch to make their model of the park so that it would be to scale.

Arturo didn't like arithmetic, but if he was going to lay out a scale model, he had to learn ratio. After he "got it," the problem wasn't so hard. Juanita learned math really quickly and helped Arturo with the park layout. "Let's calculate the whole area," she said. Mr. Moreno had brought in a drawing of the land with measurements. Once they had a scale model they could all use, they worked on drawings and layouts for the park.

Trevor painted a blue area to be a wading pool. LeDru constructed a tiny cardboard bench. Arturo used cardboard to make miniature rest rooms. Maria made trees out of small pieces of green-painted sponge on twigs. The model started to look terrific, like a real, miniature park.

Others drew a mural of kids playing on grass with flowers and slides and swings and a blue sky and white clouds. Then Maria drew a black-and-white spotted dog in the park.

"Hey, Maria," LeDru said, rinsing out the blue from his paint brush. "Dogs aren't allowed in parks!"

"Why not? I like dogs." Maria frowned at him.

Then Juanita spoke sharply. "Sure dogs can come into our park. If it's our park, we can make the rules."

Clorissa seconded Juanita's idea. "How many are in favor of letting dogs into the park?" she asked. All but four people were in favor.

"What's wrong with you guys?" Clorissa asked the four. "Probably they didn't understand. Hey, Arturo, ask them in Spanish."

So Arturo said, *"Deberíamos permitir los perros en nuestro parque?"* Then only Angel's hand remained down. "Oh, Angel, you are always against everything. But you are out voted in the democratic process," Juanita stated emphatically.

Making the model didn't keep Arturo from being impatient about the letter. On the following Wednesday LeDru said, "Maybe someone should call up the mayor's office. Maybe he forgot."

"It takes a long time for governments to do things." Clorissa sounded so sensible, as if she were teaching the class. "They have to have meetings and things."

Every morning someone asked, "Did you get a letter, Miss Fenwick?" Arturo found it hard to wait. Every day, she'd smile with amusement and say something like, "I will certainly tell you, boys and girls, if and when I hear. What we should be doing now is preparing ourselves for questions the mayor might ask."

One day, after Arturo had done all the work he could on his model, he said, "I'm tired of waiting."

"I bet the mayor won't answer at all," Angel grumbled. He stuck his hand in a bowl full of gooshy, gray papier mâché that Trevor was using to make rocks and lobbed a glob of the glop at Arturo's face. He missed, and it landed on Arturo's tee shirt, sticking to the "D" in Dodgers.

Arturo scraped the gooey wad off, glared at Angel, and strode over to him. Angel turned to run, but Arturo grabbed him by the shirttail and rubbed the mess in his hair. Several kids laughed.

"Shut up for once, *Diablo!*" Arturo twisted Angel's arm behind his back.

Miss Fenwick hadn't seen the arm-twisting, but, sensing trouble, she said, "Let's try to work together on the project, boys. Angel, here, why don't you help Trevor make some little boulders out of this papier mâché." Then she handed him a plastic bowl of the gray goop. All the kids roared with laughter, including Arturo.

The next week they still hadn't heard from the mayor. Mr. Moreno called the mayor's office to ask about the petition, and finally, within three days, a letter came.

"Hurrah!" Miss Fenwick waved the letter triumphantly. "At last it's here. You read it, Clorissa."

Clorissa read the letter in her clear, strong voice. It sounded pleased and happy in the opening. Then the letter started to say the same things that the Department of Recreation and Parks had said, that there was no money to buy the land and build a park, and that it would be several years before the city could even think of new projects.

"Several years!" Clorissa's voice was slow and heavy with disappointment.

"We'll be in high school by then." Juanita said, sounding sad.

Arturo didn't say anything. He felt let down, even though the park had been a wild idea. He had gotten to thinking they could improve things. Life sure didn't always turn out the way you wanted it to, he thought. But he didn't want to stop. Creating the design was a lot more fun when he thought it might actually become a reality. "Does that mean it's all over?" he asked.

"I told you so," shouted Angel.

LeDru jumped up from his seat behind Angel and held a fist high above him. "Give me permission to kill him, Miss Fenwick." Angel had his head on his desk with his hands over it.

"I'm afraid not, LeDru," she said with a sly smile. "It's against the rules."

"You hear that, LeDru? She's 'afraid' you can't. That means she wishes you could," Trevor said.

"Now, Trevor. You know I didn't mean that," Miss Fenwick said, but she had to put her hand over her mouth to cover an amused smile.

"We don't have to give up, do we, Mr. Moreno? Isn't there something more we can do?" Clorissa wasn't willing to quit. "Maybe we could buy the land ourselves."

Miss Fenwick's mouth flew open in surprise.

Mr. Moreno looked serious. "That would be a big project, class. But I did find out that the lady who owns the land, her name is Ethel Edmonds, will sell it for fifty-nine thousand dollars!"

There was a stunned silence.

"What?"

"Wow!"

"Nobody has that much money in the whole world!"

"We are poor."

"That's almost a million dollars!"

"It's not anywhere near a million dollars." Mr. Moreno wrote $1,000,000 on the blackboard, put $59,000 below it, and had the class subtract the difference. It was 941,000 less than a million.

"You don't have to have all the money to buy something, do you?" Trevor asked.

"No, we could probably buy it for a down payment of ten thousand dollars. Could we raise that much money?"

"That's an awful lot! My big brother bought a whole car for $250. Where would we get that much money?" LeDru wondered.

"We could do it!" Clorissa said excitedly. "We could go around the neighborhood doing jobs like taking care of a dog when its owners are at work, or painting their fence, or weeding their yard, or whatever needs to be done." She looked around eagerly. "We can do it. Can't we, guys?"

Arturo was still in shock from what the letter had said. Everyone else seemed to be, too. No one said anything for a while. "Come on, we can do it if we all work together!" Clorissa was taking charge.

Juanita held up her hand. "I'll help."

"Yeah! I will too," said LeDru.

Trevor grinned. "We can call it 'Rent-a-Kid'!"

Miss Fenwick was smiling happily. "You kids are so eager and enthusiastic. We have already learned so much. Let's continue and learn some more."

Mr. Moreno looked ready to burst with pleasure. "Great! Once again, you kids come up with such terrific ideas."

Clorissa spoke up suddenly. "Oh, and I just thought of something important. Of course we will accept donations."

There was a scattering of laughter. Arturo thought this whole project was getting pretty dumb. A bunch of kids, eleven and twelve years old, raising enough money to buy a piece of land that costs fifty-nine thousand dollars! That was super, big-time dumb.

LeDru seemed willing. "Let's see how much we can raise."

"So, okay, guys, shall I ask the owner of the land if we can have an option for four months while we try to raise the down payment?" Mr. Moreno asked.

"What's an option?" asked Juanita.

"It's an agreement between a seller and a potential buyer saying that the seller will not sell the property to anyone else for a certain length of time. The would-be buyer pays an agreed upon amount of money for this. If the would-be buyer does not 'exercise' his option within that time—like if he can't raise a down payment, he loses his money and the owner can then sell it to anyone. If he does exercise his option and buys the property, the money is included as part of the sale price."

Juanita jumped up and down. "Let's do it! Let's do it!"

"What do we have to lose?" The words popped out of Arturo and startled him. What was going on, he wondered? Why was this such . . . fun?

"Let's vote on it," Miss Fenwick suggested, and Arturo found his hand waving in the air along with those of most of the class.

Arturo walked out of the classroom at the end of the school day with Angel right behind him. He wanted to think about this crazy business. Kids buying land for a park! It was dumb. Didn't they realize that they are just little bugs, like Maria said.

Arturo's mind turned to Francisco. He hadn't seen him in a week. Just then Trevor came up. "Hey, guys, want to come over Saturday morning and help me paint our garden wall?

My parents want me to do it. They aren't offering much, but we can earn a little for ourselves and something for the park, okay?"

"Uh, I guess so." Arturo was surprised that Trevor had asked him—even for a class project. He'd never been close to Trevor— *"Blanco,"* or "Whitey," as some guys called him.

Trevor looked at Angel. "Can you come too, Angel?"

Angel turned and walked away. "Nah, I've got things to do."

It sounded like what Francisco always said, Arturo thought.

After walking a while with Trevor, Arturo asked him where he lived and when he should arrive. After Trevor had told him and had walked down the street a ways, he turned and yelled, "See you! Wear old clothes. You might get paint on them."

Old clothes? Ha! What else did he have, except for that new camouflage shirt Francisco had bought him.

CHAPTER 8

THE NEXT MORNING when Arturo got up, Mama was sitting in the living room in her blue-flowered house-coat, crying. She dabbed at her eyes with a tissue in one hand and picked nervously at the gold threads on the black couch with the other.

"What's the matter, Mama?" Arturo asked, looking into her face. It was tear streaked, and her eyes were puffy. She burst into tears, then grabbed and hugged Arturo closely. "Francisco did not come home. I am so worried. Do you know where he is?"

Seeing Mama cry made Arturo feel awful. "Where's Papa, Mama? On Saturday he doesn't go to work."

"He has gone to help your uncle with his car. Tell me, do you know where Francisco is?"

What should he say, Arturo wondered? He didn't want to scare Mama with what he thought. "Maybe he didn't want to come back late, so he stayed at a friend's house, Mama." Then he said, "Maybe he has a girlfriend."

Mama looked up with a frown. "Girlfriend? He is only fourteen, Arturo!"

"He's going to be fifteen next month, Mama."

Mama sighed, dabbed her eyes, and almost smiled. "My little baby, Francisco, my *Panchito*," she said, using his pet name.

Mama seemed to feel a little better, so Arturo grabbed a tortilla and rolled some cheese into it. "I am going to Trevor's house, Mama, to help paint a wall."

"Who? What kind of name is Trevor?"

"He's an Anglo with yellow hair, Mama. He's in my class." Arturo started out the door. "I'll be back later, Mama."

His mother sat there, red eyed but not crying. She wiped her nose with a tissue. "Be a good boy, Arturo, and come home early."

Arturo felt horrible to see his mother so upset. He couldn't have told her what he was afraid Francisco was doing. No, he couldn't. Besides, he didn't know for sure.

When Arturo turned the corner of La Luna, he saw a car coming toward him with Francisco and two guys a little older than Francisco in it. There was a little kid in the back seat; Arturo could only see the top of his head.

Arturo stared wide eyed at the car, a deep blue Chevy Monte Carlo. The car was so low it couldn't go over a beer can without dragging. What a terrific paint job! The Chevy glistened in the morning sun. There were little red lights in the back wheel wells. On the back window was printed in beautiful flourishing script: MIDNIGHT CRUISER.

The car drove slowly toward Arturo with the mufflers making a soft, deep, growling purr. Arturo felt hypnotised.

When the car reached him, Francisco opened the back door. "Good morning, little brother. Get in. We'll take you for a ride."

Arturo could hardly breathe. Imagine his big brother having friends with such class. He stared with admiration and noticed that Francisco had a new, expensive-looking watch.

Suddenly Arturo found his voice. "Francisco, Mama is worried about you. She's been crying."

"I've got a present for her to dry her tears, and one for

Papa, too, *chico.*" He held up a plastic sack. "You want a ride?"

Arturo started to step inside when the kid beside Francisco turned his head. "Yeah, man, Lobo will take you for a ride."

Angel was sitting beside his brother! Arturo felt like he had been punched in the stomach, and he frowned with annoyance.

Lobo turned slowly and looked at Arturo. His heavy, dark brows, which grew together, and the high cheekbones in his angular, unsmiling face looked menacing. Light glinted off a tiny golden crucifix dangling from his ear. He said nothing.

"Lobo is my cousin," Angel said proudly. "This is his *carro!*" Angel was really flying high, Arturo thought.

Arturo stiffened. "I gotta go over to Trevor's. We're going to paint a wall—for money." Arturo started walking off, then, suddenly remembering, he called back, "You better go see Mama, Francisco!" Angel laughed as Arturo left and said something about *"Blanco"*—"Whitey" in Spanish. He knew that Angel was laughing about Trevor and the park project, but Arturo couldn't say anything really bad to Angel with Lobo there.

When Arturo found the address on Orchard, Trevor was standing in the driveway with a paint can beside him. The wall they were supposed to paint ran along the outer edge of the driveway to the garage and was about a foot taller than Arturo.

The house was old, and white paint was peeling off its porch.

"Is this your house?"

"We're renting it while my dad finishes studying at the

university. The landlord said he'd buy the paint if we painted it."

"Man, it must be nice to have a whole house." Arturo helped spread newspapers along the edge of the wall. Trevor poured some white paint into a coffee can for Arturo. "Do you have any brothers or sisters, Trevor?" Arturo asked, dipping a brush into the paint.

"Nah, I don't have any siblings—that's what my mother calls them. She teaches psychology at the college."

"Hey, you got a real high-class family that goes to college and all. How come a rich Anglo like you is living here and going to school with us poor Latinos?" Arturo grinned like it was a joke, then ducked to avoid the punch that Trevor swung toward him with his free hand.

"I'm not rich, but I am mean, so look out!" Trevor took another swipe with his other fist.

As they painted, Trevor told him that he felt like an outsider. He was always the last chosen to play soccer at school, and after school no one asked him to play stickball.

"So where is there to play?"

"I've seen you guys playing on a roof on La Luna."

"Yeah, sometimes we play catch on the roof of my apartment building, but it's a dud; we keep losing balls." Arturo was surprised: Trevor wasn't all that bad when you got to know him. They talked a lot, and the morning disappeared rapidly. At about one o'clock Trevor's mother called them in for peanut-butter sandwiches and soup. By four o'clock the wall was completed, though Arturo was hot and sweaty and glad to be through.

After wiping the sweat off his forehead with a clean rag, he rinsed his paintbrush in water and wiped it dry with the rag.

"I'll go get your money." Trevor disappeared into the house while Arturo put lids back on the cans. The white wall gleamed in the sun, so pure and clean—like a new beginning. Funny, it made the whole yard look better. There was an orange tree by the garage, partway in front of the wall. Arturo noticed what a great picture its bright round oranges, small white starflowers, and bright green leaves made against the white background. He had helped to make that picture. The thought startled him. He could shape things the way he wanted them and make them look good. He liked the feeling.

After Trevor paid Arturo, he stuck the money into his pocket and gave Trevor a punch on the arm. "Thanks, *Blanco!* See you at school, man." As Arturo waved and walked off, he decided that Trevor really wasn't bad at all.

On Thursday in class Mr. Moreno talked with them about the park project. He told the class that he had met with the owner of the land, Mrs. Edmonds. When he asked if she would be willing not to sell the lot to anyone for four months, she suggested that they sign a legal option to buy instead of having an informal agreement. Mr. Moreno had explained that they had no money to secure such an option, but Mrs. Edmonds said she was willing to accept a minimal amount of fifty dollars!

"I had to leave it there, guys. I guess our next step is to raise that fifty dollars!"

Now the kids got busy. Arturo had made big banners to put on the school buses. They said, "RENT-A-KID, BUY-A-PARK!" in huge letters, then, "Weeding, baby-sitting, pet care, car washing, anything!" in smaller letters. "It's like free advertising," said Juanita.

The next Monday the kids brought money they had earned over the weekend. Juanita had watered Señora Montez's houseplants and fed her cat while she visited her married daughter in El Monte. Clorissa had baby-sat her nephew one afternoon. One kid had washed his father's car, and someone else had "chicken-sat" his uncle's fifteen chickens while the family went away for the weekend. LeDru had pulled weeds for the man next door and got a dollar and thirty-five cents from bottles he found in the street. Angel hadn't done anything. "How much did we get?" Arturo asked. Although he found it hard to give up money he had earned, Arturo donated fifteen of the eighteen dollars he had been paid for painting.

LeDru counted the money and found that they had $87.50.

Juanita moaned. "Even if we earn one hundred dollars a week, it will take us forever to earn enough for the down payment." She put her hands up to her face and made whimpering noises. "It would take about a month less than two years to raise ten thousand dollars, and we probably wouldn't work every week!" She sobbed dramatically. "We only have four months!"

"That was good calculating, Juanita." Miss Fenwick was always reminding them of education, Arturo thought. She was looking at the money spread on her desk while Maria rolled it into paper tubes.

"Are there other things we can do to raise money besides this?" Arturo asked.

"We can make cookies to sell!" Maria spoke up suddenly. She hardly ever spoke in class. Everyone looked surprised.

"Maybe some people would just give us money if they knew about our park project," Juanita suggested.

"Yeah, we can use all the help we can get!" said LeDru.

"Right! Some jobs are too big to do all by yourself." Trevor talked rapidly. "We would never have a space program or anything really big, my dad says, if a whole bunch of people didn't work together."

The ideas seemed to please Mr. Moreno. "So how could we let people know what we are doing?"

"When grown-ups plan big projects like this, they have fund-raising events." Clorissa sounded like an official who had been doing this kind of work for years. "I read about things like that sometimes. Maybe we could get an article in the newspaper!"

Juanita clapped loudly, LeDru yelled, "All right, Clorissa!" and lots of others cheered.

"Right, Clorissa. What is it called when somebody gets an article in the paper that will help create interest in a project?" Whenever there was a chance to learn something, Miss Fenwick got excited.

"Publicity!" Trevor shot back.

"Why don't you call the newspaper, Mr. Moreno?" Once again Arturo felt his heart pounding faster. They had all worked too hard to see their project die.

"All right, I will." Mr. Moreno smiled broadly and raised a fist into the air. "But—"

Miss Fenwick interrupted quickly. "I think a member of the class should call, and that you boys and girls should talk to the reporter if one comes to interview us."

Most of the kids turned to each other and smiled with a kind of nervous excitement. Then voices rose. "We will, we will!"

Arturo swallowed hard at the thought of talking to a reporter. He couldn't do that. He would just stay out of the way and let the others do it. Talk to somebody who would take your words and put them in a newspaper? No way, he thought. That was scary. He would stutter and wouldn't be able to think of anything at all.

"Especially they can talk to Clorissa," someone called out.

"I would be pleased to speak to a reporter." Clorissa was always so grown-up. Nothing seemed to make her nervous or upset.

Mr. Moreno made an "O" for okay with his upheld hand. "Since you suggested doing other things, why don't you call the newspaper, Arturo?"

"Uh, no, I don't really want to. How about Trevor?"

"Sure!" Trevor spoke up eagerly. "I'll call them."

"It's a deal!" Mr. Moreno winked.

When Arturo left school that day, he felt happy again. But were they all being fools? They had less than four months to raise the money for the down payment! As he left school, he saw Angel leaving, too, and he hurried to get ahead of him. He didn't want to be anywhere near him.

CHAPTER 9

WHEN ARTURO GOT HOME, Francisco was there, and Mama was all smiles. She showed Arturo her new blouse with orange and blue parrots on it that Francisco had bought for her.

"Francisco was at his friend's house for the weekend." Mama smiled at Arturo, then put her arm around Francisco's neck and gave him a kiss on the cheek.

"Yeah, we forgot about the time, so I stayed over at Lobo—I mean, Juan's house."

"You're a good boy, Francisco. I hope your friends are, too." Mama gave him a squeeze, then let him go. When Arturo looked at Francisco, his brother glanced down at the floor. He wasn't wearing his gold chain and earring.

Arturo noticed that his father wasn't smiling. He could see that Papa doubted that Francisco's friends were good. Before dinner Arturo had a chance to talk to Francisco alone. "Hey, thanks for the camouflage shirt, Francisco. When are you going to let me join the *Vatos,* too? Angel said Lobo said he could join after the end of the school year. Maybe if you talked to Lobo . . ."

Francisco leaned back on the bed with his hands behind his head, his eyes half closed. "When the time is right, we will tell you. For now . . ." He put a finger up to his lips to indicate silence.

Arturo smiled. Francisco was some brother! He could hardly wait for the *Vatos* to let him in.

After dinner Arturo sat down at the kitchen table and started doing his arithmetic. Papa would approve of that. Miss Fenwick had given them a whole list of story problems to solve to figure out how much money they could make in a certain amount of time in order to put a down payment on the park. Arithmetic wasn't usually interesting, but this was for something real. Arturo even thought of talking to Papa about it but decided not to.

Then he thought of the newspaper. Why would the paper send a reporter out to their class to talk to them? They weren't important enough to be news. News was when somebody was elected president or an airplane crashed.

"Papa, do you think that a newspaper would send a reporter out to talk to our class about getting a park?"

Papa turned on the old black-and-white TV. "Are you still dreaming about that foolishness, *mijo?* I tell you what; if a reporter comes to your class, I will stand on my head in the living room."

Arturo laughed at the thought of his father standing on his head. "I would like to see that, Papa! Do you really think you could do it?"

"I won't need to. No one is going to come to your school for any craziness like that."

Arturo chuckled and went back to the arithmetic. Maybe all that would happen is that he would learn arithmetic. But he could still hardly wait to find out what the newspaper said to Trevor.

The next morning in school everyone wanted to know what the newspaper had told Trevor, but he wasn't there yet.

Miss Fenwick kept looking at the door, waiting for Trevor. Arturo could see that she was excited, but she just smiled as she always did and said, "Don't forget that the most important reason we are here is to learn things that will help us through our whole life."

"But where is Trevor?" Clorissa asked impatiently.

Miss Fenwick took one last look at the door, then said, "Clorissa, let's talk about why we need a park and how people can help us get one. If a reporter comes, you boys and girls have to speak to him or her."

"Yeah, you can't just stand there and look dumb and say, 'duhh, uhhh.'" LeDru opened his mouth and rolled his head around.

Arturo turned his head in an attempt to escape the whole idea. He would hate it, just hate it, if a reporter talked to him. He wouldn't even be able to answer. He felt his hands turn cold just thinking about it.

Miss Fenwick divided them into groups. In each group one person was the reporter and three were students. Then someone else took a turn being the reporter. Finally, each group told the class what their questions and answers were.

Right in the middle of the exercise, Trevor came in, grinning and wiggling his eyebrows up and down. "Yes, yes, they are sending a reporter over at two o'clock this afternoon!" he said before he even sat down.

"Yea!" "Yippee!" Kids jumped up from their seats and hopped around. Clorissa stood up proudly, then raised her arm in a cheer. "Hurray!"

"They really are?" Arturo burst into giggles as he imagined his father standing on his head.

"I want all of you to have something ready to say to the reporter. Who will be our main spokesperson?" Miss Fenwick asked.

The class nominated Clorissa, Juanita, and Trevor, but

when they voted, the winner was Clorissa by a landslide. Clorissa stood up, gave a quick mock bow, opened her big dark eyes wide, and smiled. "Thank you, fellow classmates, for this vote of trust."

Everyone laughed.

Once Clorissa was chosen, Arturo felt pretty safe that he wouldn't have to say anything. But as two o'clock approached, people must have been getting fidgety because they were moving their chairs around a lot. Arturo's stomach felt funny, and he kept looking at the clock. He would try to stay out of the way once the interview got started.

A little after two o'clock, there was a knock on the door, and Miss Fenwick let in two reporters, a white man and a pretty young black woman. Then Miss Fenwick had the class answer some questions.

"There's a lot of artwork here—a mural—and who did this site plan?" asked the man.

"Arturo," Juanita said, pointing to him. He turned his head away. His face got as hot as a chili pepper.

Then they all walked together to the site for the park. Clorissa walked beside the woman reporter. Arturo was way in back, but he wanted to hear what they were saying. Gradually he moved up until he was behind them. He heard Clorissa say, "Helping create this park would be a real accomplishment for me. I could look back and think, 'I was part of making this happen. My efforts came through.'" Striding along in her jeans and blue Dodgers jacket, she sounded and looked almost like a reporter herself.

At the lot, the reporters and the class wandered through the trash. "Do you think your class can make this dump into a park?" the male reporter asked Angel.

Angel narrowed his eyes. "Nah!" Arturo could tell he

was trying to look cool. "And even if we did, the hoods around here would break up the slides and write all over stuff."

The reporter scribbled in his notepad.

Juanita was standing by Angel, frowning angrily.

"Why do you want to create a park here when you won't even be at this school next year to use it?"

"I don't want to make the park. I think it's dumb," Angel said. He was really showing off. Arturo could see Juanita getting angry. She boldly stepped up to the reporter. "We are doing it for the little kids who will still be here. Some are our sisters and brothers. We want them to have a safe place to play."

Arturo moved right up beside Juanita. "Tell him about the fish heads, Juanita."

"Yeah, tell them about the fish heads," said LeDru.

The reporter scribbled away rapidly while Arturo stood smiling at Juanita as she talked. He liked her big strong ideas.

When she finished, she was excited and out of breath. Then she saw Arturo looking at her, and she closed her eyes with embarrassment.

As Clorissa and the female reporter walked through the junked cars, hunks of old carpet, and bottles, the woman asked, "Whose cars are these? How did they get here?"

"They used to belong to people in the neighborhood. When the cars don't work anymore, people put them here because they don't know what else to do with them."

The lady reporter waved her hands around. "You think you can make a park out of this? It's really a dump. You're just kids."

"Yes, it is a mess," Clorissa said. She wasn't a bit bothered by the question. "But if we all work hard together, we can do it."

The reporter smiled and wrote down Clorissa's words.

The male reporter asked Miss Fenwick if she didn't think it was a bad idea to get the kids' hopes up by taking on such a big project that had such a small chance of working out.

"We don't have unrealistic hopes," Miss Fenwick said. "We have learned a lot already about property, government, mathematics—about how to speak up and express ourselves clearly in person and on paper."

"We talk about our chances of winning or losing," Mr. Moreno said. "The kids know it might not work out. Living in this neighborhood, they are used to seeing things not working."

Arturo was getting more and more excited. After all, this wasn't just any man and woman asking questions. They were going to tell thousands of people—heck, maybe millions—about the park project. He forgot that he didn't like to speak up in a group or to have people look at him and burst out, "Yeah, we're used to things not working, but sometimes even kids get fed up and we . . . we . . ." Suddenly Arturo realized he had spoken to the reporter.

"Aren't you the boy who did the park design?" The reporter was writing down everything he had just said. "Arturo Morales?"

Arturo felt flustered and looked at his shoe as it scuffed up a gust of dirt. Then he found his voice again. "Yeah. We don't want to leave this place . . . all messy. Wouldn't it be nice if, when people come to Los Angeles from other countries, they come and see our park all clean and nice and they think, . . ." Arturo's throat was dry, and his heart was beating rapidly. "They will think . . . this is the way America is!"

Angel and Maria stood watching intently.

The reporters put away their pads, and the man said, "Let's take a few pictures, now." He put Arturo and Angel by a couple of wrecked cars. Arturo tried to move away from Angel, but the man kept saying, "Stand closer!" Then they took a bunch of combination photos of the kids and the teachers.

On the way back to school, Mr. Moreno and Miss Fenwick had trouble keeping everybody in lines. Arturo bounced and skipped, and now and then LeDru or Trevor punched him and he punched back playfully. Kids yelled, "When are we going to be in the paper?" "When can we see the story?" "How could you say all that stuff, Clorissa. I would have been so scared!"

Now and then Arturo laughed out loud to himself. He couldn't wait to see Papa standing on his head.

CHAPTER 10

TO ARTURO, waiting for the newspaper article to be published was like waiting for Christmas.

On the next Wednesday, Trevor, Juanita, Clorissa, and some others brought in newspapers. Juanita skipped and waved her copy of the paper. "Can I read the article, Miss Fenwick? Can I?"

"Certainly, Juanita."

Juanita flipped her long dark hair over her shoulder. Pushing her glasses up her nose, she read in a tiny voice. "A Class with Lots on Its Mind." She giggled. "That's funny, isn't it?"

"So read it!" LeDru yelled.

The article began by describing the junk on the dump. "They forgot the old rusted-out mufflers," yelled Angel. Then it talked about how the sixth graders of Southwood Elementary School were trying to clean it up and make it into a park. Juanita read Miss Fenwick's words. " 'I think young people should have a say in the community. They can do a lot more for it if we let them.' The park project, Fenwick says, has brought out strengths and talents in the students that they probably didn't know they possessed. 'I see such determination on their part to fight for what they want.' "

There was a lot of cheering, and Arturo yelled, "Yea, Miss Fenwick!"

"That's neat!" said Trevor.

Clorissa said, "That sounds like it came out of a book, Miss Fenwick!"

Miss Fenwick's cheeks got pink, and she looked down at her desk. "Thank you, Clorissa."

The rest of the story explained that the class had less than four months to raise money for the down payment on the lot. Juanita smiled proudly and sat down.

Arturo thought the pictures looked great. There he was in front of a bunch of kids, Clorissa in back looking over his shoulder. Angel didn't care anything about the park project but had crowded in front to get his picture taken.

Arturo waved his hand at Miss Fenwick. "My father was so sure the reporter wouldn't come that he said he would stand on his head if she did." Arturo burst out laughing.

"So did he do it?" Trevor wanted to know.

"Kind of," Arturo said, still laughing. "He slid off the sofa backward with his head down. Mama held his legs up about a second, then he fell sideways onto the floor and yelled, 'Woaooo.'" Arturo choked with laughter and rubbed his eyes, which were watering, while he thought of the part he didn't tell: how Papa had yelled, 'Help, I'm blind!' when his shirt fell over his face; the sight of his big, lace-up work boots waving in the air and his bare belly sticking out; and then how Mrs. Lopez, two of her kids, and Maria had peeked through the kitchen door, and how Mrs. Lopez had seemed frightened and had yelled, *"Qué pasa?"*

Everyone laughed. Maria giggled quietly. She had been there and had seen Arturo's father.

After everyone calmed down, Mr. Moreno slapped his hands together loudly. "So! What do we do next?"

"There must be ways we can raise more money," Trevor

said. "Maybe we could have a benefit. People do that for charities."

"What's a benefit?" LeDru asked, puzzled.

"Benefit means help," Juanita explained.

"You give a dinner or put on a play or something. People buy tickets to come or maybe they buy chances on a prize. All the money goes to help the charity." Trevor sat up, eager and alert. "What can we do for a benefit?"

The class decided a dinner would cost too much, and besides, where would they have it? "How about a dance?" asked Maria.

Then Juanita said, "How would a dance raise money? If it's for us kids—we don't have any money—and how would we give a dance for grown-ups? Why don't we make cookies and sell them?"

Someone said they were all too young for a dance. Maria glanced sideways from her half-closed eyes and said, "I don't think so."

LeDru yelled, "Boo! Boo! Who wants to dance anyway? How about a softball game?" He grinned wildly. It was a great idea, Arturo thought. Several people looked at LeDru with surprise.

"That could be a winner, LeDru," Miss Fenwick said. "We might be able to have it in the school yard."

"Let's vote on it," Clorissa suggested. "I think that is a very intelligent idea."

The idea passed overwhelmingly. "When is this intelligent softball game going to take place?" asked Angel.

"We have a little less than four months to raise that money. We'd better have the game a week from this Saturday!" Clorissa sounded like a politician, Arturo thought.

"Let's pick the teams now." The softball game sounded like fun to Arturo.

"The team that gets LeDru has to take Juanita, too!" Angel said, laughing wildly.

Seeing Juanita look as though she were going to cry, Arturo quickly said, "Why don't we have a cookie sale, too, like Juanita suggested?" He glanced over to see her smiling.

Everyone thought the cookie sale was a great idea, and they appointed Juanita chairperson. Trevor was voted to be in charge of the game. They also decided to make a flyer to tell people about the game. Clorissa would write in English on one side of the flyer, and Arturo would illustrate it and translate the words into Spanish on the other side. Maria and two other kids would mail them out, and some of the boys would deliver them to homes and businesses. Angel was appointed to get and return the softball, the bats, and the other equipment.

"Oh, all right," he said, sulkily.

When school let out that day, everyone knew exactly what to do. Arturo already had ideas for the design of the flyer. Miss Fenwick said she'd ask for permission to use the playground.

When he left the school building, Arturo avoided Angel again and hurried home eagerly. Jumping up the steps two at a time, he stepped carefully around the Lopez kids' toys and bounded through the door of his apartment.

Once inside, he saw his mother kneeling beside her bed, fingering her rosary beads. He could hear her saying a Hail Mary. On the dresser was a lighted votive candle flickering in a red glass holder in front of a picture of the Virgin Mary.

No one else was home.

"Mama, is something wrong? Where is Papa? What is it?"

"Oh, *mijo*, it is so terrible." His mother's eyes were red. She started crying. She wrapped her arms around Arturo, put her face on his shoulder, and sobbed.

"What is it, Mama?"

"It's Francisco. He and Papa had a terrible fight. Papa came home early and found Francisco lying on his bed, smoking a funny-smelling cigarette. It was marijuana. When your father asked him why he wasn't at work at the auto-body shop, Francisco said . . ." His mother broke down again.

Arturo had an idea of what was coming. "Mama, what did he say?"

"He said he didn't work at an auto shop and . . ." Through her sobs, Mama finally got out that Francisco had said he used drugs whenever he wanted to and that he belonged to *Los Vatos Locos.* "He told your father he worked with them, 'doing whatever there is to do.'"

Mama made the sign of the cross, lifted her eyes to heaven, and asked the Virgin to help her. *"Madre de Dios ayúdame!"* she pleaded. "And then he . . . he . . . he . . . told Papa that he . . . ," she choked and could hardly continue, "would never be such a fool as Papa was. He would never waste his time doing stupid work that any donkey could do." Mama wiped her eyes.

"That's when Papa hit Francisco hard across the face and told him to leave his home." Mama calmed down and told him that Francisco had taken only a coat and a small sack of things. Then Papa went out—maybe to Balo's for a *cerveza* and to talk to his friends.

Arturo sat in the darkened bedroom with his mother. He

felt as though he had received a hard blow. He could hardly remember what he had been happy about when he came home. Mama was praying quietly again while the flickering red light of the candle writhed over the walls and ceiling.

CHAPTER 11

AFTER FRANCISCO MOVED OUT, Mama hardly smiled at all. It made Arturo sad. Papa was gloomy, too, but Arturo felt sure that Francisco was all right. He knew how to take care of himself, and his *compañeros* would help him. That's what gangs were for. The guys were like brothers who took care of each other, no matter what. Arturo could hardly wait to join.

At least Miss Fenwick was always cheerful, Arturo thought as he hurried off to school. Since they had been working on the park project, the whole class seemed happy. About halfway down La Luna, Arturo noticed Maria coming from their apartment building. He sped up, but it was too late.

"Hey, Arturo!" She ran toward him.

He was caught again. Arturo groaned. That Maria! She stuck to him like a wad of chewing gum. She must really like him. What a pest she was. Arturo couldn't walk out of the apartment without finding her standing around waiting for him.

"How do you like my ribbons, Arturo?" She beamed. Maria's hair was divided into two long curly tails, one on each side of her face. "I got them at Buy-Rite last Saturday." She held up one red-ribboned tail for inspection.

"Yeah, they're nice." Arturo looked away and walked on.

She smiled sidewise, then started in about how one of her cousins had a new boyfriend and another cousin was getting married.

"She's sixteen! That's only four years older than I am."
Maria looked Arturo directly in the face.

"Is she going to finish high school?"

"What for?" Maria half closed her dark eyes. "School
isn't any fun. She's going to have a big wedding." She took
a breath.

Arturo frowned. What a pest. What a bore. Maria never
talked about anything but clothes and junk. Now she was
babbling about her aunt having a baby and that maybe she
could earn enough money baby-sitting her nephews and
nieces to buy a new dress for sixth-grade graduation in June.
"They have some fantastic ones at Buy-Rite with lace, and
white lace tights to go with them, and . . ."

Arturo stopped listening. Maria sounded like Angel, talking about how dumb school was. Suddenly he had a great
idea. "Maria," he said and smiled mischievously. "Guess
who told me he likes you?"

Maria stopped talking and stared, hypnotized, at Arturo.
"Who?"

Arturo felt devilishly happy about his idea and wanted
to laugh out loud. "Angel."

"Angel?" Maria seemed to like the idea. Arturo certainly hoped so. He put a hand over his mouth to keep
from laughing.

When they got to school, Arturo dashed into the boy's
rest room to escape Maria. When he came out, he walked
down the hall slowly to his class. By the office door he saw
Miss Fenwick. Then he heard a woman's angry voice practically shouting. "You are crazy! You are taking advantage of
those kids for some goofy reason of your own. You know
they can't do anything that big. You are leading them to disappointment and disillusionment."

80

Arturo stopped in his tracks by the door. Miss Fenwick's quiet voice responded. "You are entitled to your opinion, but I think I'll see how the principal feels about this."

When he heard footsteps coming toward the door, Arturo hurried down the hall. He didn't want to be caught listening, so he walked quickly toward his classroom. A few other kids were already there, talking excitedly about plans for the softball game. But Arturo was thinking about Miss Fenwick being called crazy. It bothered him.

When Miss Fenwick arrived a couple minutes after the bell, she wasn't wearing her usual smile. Arturo stared hard at her eyes. They were red, like Mama's had been lately. She'd been crying, he decided. Seeing that made him uncomfortable and unhappy, the way he felt when he saw Mama crying. Glancing around the room, he saw Clorissa and Juanita frowning at one another. They seemed puzzled.

Clorissa got up quietly and went up to Miss Fenwick. She put her hand on her teacher's back and leaned over and whispered in her ear. Clorissa was bigger than Miss Fenwick, and standing beside her, she looked like a mother comforting her child.

"Thank you, Clorissa. I'm all right. I've just had a rather unpleasant experience." Miss Fenwick looked up at the class. While Clorissa went back to her seat, Miss Fenwick sniffed briskly, wiped her nose with a tissue, and forced a smile. "Class, I told the administrators about our project and asked if we could use the playground for our softball game. Most of them didn't approve when they heard what it was for." She paused a moment. "The lady in charge said it was not good to encourage you boys and girls on such a big project because you would be disappointed and unhappy if it failed." Miss Fenwick was in control now, Arturo could tell. "She has a good point. How do you feel about that?"

"Yeah, she's right!" Angel yelled from the back. "It's dumb to think we can get a park."

Juanita jumped up angrily. "Miss Fenwick, don't listen to Angel. I've been learning lots of stuff for this project, and I think it's great, what we are trying to do, and . . . and . . . I think it's wonderful how you are helping, and . . . can't we have our ball game?" She flopped down while the class clapped.

Clorissa put her hand up. "My friend Vanetta is a really good runner and wins all kinds of ribbons for the fifty-yard dash at her high school. She says you can't worry about failing when you want to do something. She's lost lots of races, but she says that if she thought about losing, she might never even have tried in the first place. Then she wouldn't have won any races or prizes. I think we should try—like Vanetta does."

Clorissa's words made Arturo more eager to try even harder. He wanted to win races—or something—like Clorissa's friend. The words, "Yeah, let's keep at it!" popped out of him before he even thought.

Miss Fenwick looked up with a faint smile. She seemed a lot happier. "You are such intelligent, talented, hardworking boys and girls. Yes, we can still have our benefit, if you want it. After I was refused, I went to Mrs. Wentworth, the principal. She said it was unrealistic to expect that we could buy the lot for a park but that the softball game would be good for the school and the community whether it raised any money or not."

"Good! You didn't give up either, Miss Fenwick," Trevor said.

"But we want to get money for the park," Arturo said.

"As long as we've started it, let's go for it!" said LeDru.

"Yeahhhh!" The kids all cheered. They voted "yes" on whether or not to go ahead with the softball game on Saturday. It was official. Full steam ahead! Arturo felt really charged up.

A few days after their article came out in the paper, people began to respond. Miss Fenwick walked into class carrying a bundle of letters.

"Look, boys and girls. These are all for us!" She handed out letters. "Each of you open one and read it aloud."

The letters were from people who had read the article and wanted to help. Arturo opened a letter and out fell a check. "Hey, look, a check for twenty dollars!" Arturo waved it joyfully to an eruption of cheers and hand clapping. He read the letter but had trouble with some of the words at the end, so Juanita helped him with the last line.

"It says, 'I earnestly hope that your ten . . . uh, ten . . . tenacity and diligence will enable you to succeed in your endeavor.' What does tena . . . tenacity mean?" Juanita asked.

Arturo felt better that Juanita didn't know all the words. Maybe he wasn't so dumb after all. He rolled the words around in his head: Tenacity. Endeavor. He liked the sound of them.

"It means sticking to something and not giving up," Clorissa stated with assurance. "My friend Vanetta has tenacity."

"That's exactly what it means," Miss Fenwick said. "And it describes all of you." She was back to her optimistic self.

All the letters wished the class well, some with plain

words and some with fancy words. Most of the letters included checks or paper money.

"How much did we get altogether?" Angel was actually interested.

"Why don't you count it, Angel." Miss Fenwick put the pile of checks and cash on his desk. He counted quietly, then announced, "Two hundred and seventy-five dollars!"

More cheers and hand clapping.

"When people are kind enough to donate money to us for our project, we should write letters to thank them," Miss Fenwick said. She spoke for a few moments about politeness, gratitude, and how to write a thank-you letter. After discussing what to write, the class divided the letters and settled down to write thank-you notes.

After the letter-writing session, Miss Fenwick said, "We need someone to take care of this money and keep records on it."

"I'll take it!" Angel said and started folding it to put into his pocket.

"No way!" LeDru said. He stepped over to Angel on his long legs and took the money. "I'd sooner trust a hungry dog with hamburger." Everyone laughed while he carried the checks and paper money over to Miss Fenwick's desk.

"Maybe we should put it in the bank," Juanita suggested.

"Wonderful idea, Juanita," said Miss Fenwick. Then they had a long discussion on banks. They asked, What do banks do? How do they do it? Why not just keep the money in a box? How do you open an account?

"I haven't had to worry about keeping money safe until now," LeDru said. "When can we start our bank account?"

Having a real bank account sounded terrific to Arturo.

"Let's open one on Thursday when Mr. Moreno is here,"

Miss Fenwick said, returning to their lesson about banks and how to use them. Next she gave them an arithmetic assignment about decimals and place value and percent in figuring interest, which was important to know if you wanted to manage your money.

"If we are going to have a treasurer to take care of our money, what should his or her qualifications be?" Miss Fenwick asked.

"Good at arithmetic," said LeDru.

"And honest!" Maria said.

"And I think that it is extremely important for a treasurer to be neat and well organized," Clorissa said.

"Okay, let's see how you all did on the arithmetic problems. Trade papers with your neighbor, and we'll grade them."

Arturo didn't really get the idea of decimals and place and goofed up the problems. He got sixty percent — a D. Papa would be disappointed if he saw a grade like that. He was always telling Arturo how important it was for any kind of job to know numbers.

When all the papers were graded, they learned that Juanita had the highest grade, a ninety-seven. Trevor was next with a ninety-five.

"I nominate Juanita for treasurer," said Clorissa while Juanita squirmed and twisted in her seat with embarrassment.

Somebody else nominated Trevor, but Juanita won the vote.

"Our new treasurer," Clorissa said with a flourish of her hand.

"Speech! Speech!" said Trevor.

Juanita stood up and giggled. Then she spoke seriously.

"I'll try to be a good treasurer and keep track of the money and stuff. And, oh yeah, I'll be honest." She giggled some more, covered her mouth, and sat down.

"Let's be ready to go to the bank on Thursday, class. I'll see you tomorrow." Miss Fenwick closed her notebook and got up to leave.

As Arturo was walking home that afternoon, he heard a familiar sound behind him. It was the Midnight Cruiser, and there was Francisco in the front seat on the passenger's side. He leaned out the window. *"Hola, chico, qué pasa?"*

"Francisco, what's happening with you? Hey, man, we miss you. Mama is so worried." He was in such high spirits about class and was about to tell Francisco what had happened when he remembered that Francisco would probably just make fun of it.

"Get in. We'll go for a ride and talk."

As they drove around, Francisco talked, and Arturo listened. And there was Lobo, driving. The guy in the backseat kept looking out the side window, and Arturo couldn't see his face.

"Things are okay, *chico*. Tell Mama I'm staying with Lobo. I'm busy, and we're all taking care of each other. Tell her and Papa not to worry."

"So, you want to join us, too, eh?" Lobo said, looking around at Arturo. His eyes were covered by dark glasses, but a slow smile curved his mouth. "Maybe soon, huh?"

Arturo swelled up with pride. "I—"

Francisco turned quickly and said, "He's just a *niño*," and reached out and ruffled Arturo's hair.

"I'm not either, Francisco. I'm going to graduate from sixth grade this June."

"How's your crazy park project going?"

Arturo fell silent. He didn't want to talk about it with the *Vatos*. They would think it was sissy stuff. But he said, "Some reporters came and talked to us and put stuff in the paper about it with my picture, too." Arturo started talking rapidly. He told how people had sent money and said, "We're having a softball game this Saturday to raise more money. Can you come, Francisco?"

"Yeah, well, we'll see, *chico*. You go do your homework. I'll be in touch." Lobo pulled the Cruiser up to the curb while Francisco reached back and opened the door for his brother. "Here, *chico*, buy something for yourself and for Mama." Francisco shoved a paper bill into Arturo's hand.

Arturo got out, waved to Francisco, and stood at the curb while the deep, velvet purr of the Cruiser's muffler faded in the distance.

He was puzzled. Francisco didn't sound like himself at all. "How is the park project?" "Do your homework!" Something weird was going on. He looked down at the crisp bill in his hand. Twenty dollars!

A strange mixture of feelings surged through Arturo. When Lobo invited Arturo to join, Francisco had messed things up for him and called him a *niño* in front of Lobo. Francisco didn't want to share the fun and money, Arturo thought. He didn't even care about Arturo's picture in the paper. Arturo felt annoyed with him in spite of all the money he had given him.

CHAPTER
12

THE LETTERS KEPT COMING IN with checks for five and ten dollars, even a couple for a hundred. On Thursday morning, Juanita stood up in class and read a progress report.

"Trevor washed his father's car. Maria took care of her nephews. LeDru picked up bottles and cans for $2.15." She pushed a strand of hair off her glasses. "That makes $754.15. Most of it is in checks, but some is here, in real money." She patted a red coffee can on her desk.

The whole class gasped. That was a lot of money! A shiver went through Arturo.

"Wow!" someone said. "You could buy a neat car for that!"

They clapped and hooted.

"Let's put it in the bank, class!" Mr. Moreno took a couple of springy steps in his athletic shoes, as if he wanted to leap over the desk.

Miss Fenwick had told the bank manager that the class was coming that morning. "Since the bank is only a few blocks from school, I got permission for us to walk down there," she told them.

When they started out, everyone bounced around but stayed in pretty good lines. Arturo carried the cash in the red coffee can and walked beside Juanita. LeDru carried the checks in an envelope.

The traffic seemed like a wild, rushing river of trucks

and cars to Arturo while he and the class waited for the light to change.

The sign on the bank's door said, *"Abra aquí su cuenta de ahorros."* "Hey, Miss Fenwick, it says 'Open your savings account here,'" said Juanita.

Arturo felt scared and important all at the same time. There were a few customers in the bank, and they turned to stare at the flock of over thirty kids.

Miss Fenwick spoke to the bank manager, who came out of his office and shook hands with each kid. He gave them a tour of the bank and told them what was going on in each area. Then he led them to the "New Accounts" desk, where a lady helped the class open their account.

Mr. Moreno gave handfuls of change from the coffee can to the kids. "Here, make stacks of a dollar each."

An old lady with a red suit and a cane walked by Maria and Angel, who sat on the marble floor stacking up dimes and nickels. "Where did you children get all that money? And what are you going to do with it?"

"We want to build a park in our neighborhood," Maria said.

"What a nice idea. Suppose I add a little to it?" She walked over to Clorissa, who was counting the paper money, and handed her a ten-dollar bill.

"That is very generous of you," said Clorissa, and suddenly the high-vaulted room echoed with a chorus of thank-yous.

After the account was opened and Juanita and Miss Fenwick had signed the signature card, Juanita said, "You mean I can really write checks?"

"Only if it's for our park project and if I sign, too," Miss

Fenwick said with a laugh. Juanita did three little dance skips and whirled with joy.

Arturo watched her. Juanita was some *chica!* As they walked back, Arturo asked, "How come you're better at arithmetic than me?"

"I don't know. How come you are so good at printing and drawing, and I'm not?" Juanita wrinkled her nose and looked away.

Juanita had the tip of her long brown pigtail curled to-day. It looked pretty, Arturo thought.

Back in class, Arturo started working on the handbill an-nouncing the game. He drew a boy hitting a ball and a girl jumping to catch it. He wrote in English on one side and in Spanish on the other: "HELP US BUILD A PARK!" *"¡AYÚDANOS A CONSTRUIR UN PARQUE!"* The sign told about the softball teams, *Las Lunas* and *Las Estrellas,* or The Moons and The Stars. "Donation $1.50," he wrote.

After LeDru and three others returned from posting the notices on people's mailboxes and in Julio's *mercado* on La Luna, the class picked teams. Mr. Moreno was the coach of *Las Lunas,* and Miss Fenwick coached *Las Estrellas.* They tossed a coin to see who got LeDru. He was the best at any sport.

LeDru went to the *Estrellas.* Clorissa was second, cho-sen by the *Lunas,* then Trevor was chosen. At the end some-one yelled, "Hey, whoever takes Juanita gets a handicap."

"They sure do!" yelled someone else.

"I'm good at arithmetic," she yelled back and made a face.

Finally Saturday arrived, and all the kids congregated at the playground. The *Lunas* had white caps, and the *Estrellas* had blue ones. Players who didn't have caps put a piece of white or blue crepe paper around their right arm.

Clorissa stood at home plate, test-swinging a bat. She looked like a pro with her white sweatshirt and cap. "Move over, Darryl Strawberry," she said. "I'm going to beat your record."

Arturo and Angel helped Juanita take two tables out of the cafeteria for the bake-sale items she was putting out.

Arturo had convinced Mama to make her best chocolate cake with the frosting that she poured on hot so that it soaked right in.

Lots of parents, and even other people from the neighborhood, brought baked goods. Maria's mother brought white-frosted cupcakes with rainbow-colored candy sprinkles. Another lady brought *pan dulce* with bright pink frosting. Mrs. Lopez made chocolate-chip cookies that sold before she even put them on the table. Another lady brought tamales that smelled so delicious that Arturo's mouth watered.

He looked at the table spread with tempting things, then looked around but saw only a few ladies who had brought cakes and cookies. It was about 4:30, the time the game was supposed to start. Weren't they going to have an audience? Arturo had been hoping that Francisco would come. He had said he might.

"No one's going to come to watch a bunch of dumb kids who can't even play ball," yelled Angel.

"Shut up, Angel!"

Arturo was surprised. Clorissa was usually so polite. She towered over Angel and glared down at him.

"Yeah, shut up!" a bunch of others echoed.

Angel looked up at Clorissa and shut up.

At about 4:45, people started showing up. Lots of fathers had to work on Saturdays and were just getting home. Arturo looked at each new arrival but didn't see Francisco. He grinned proudly when he saw Papa and Mama and jounced back and forth eagerly. He wanted to run from base to base just for them.

More neighbors and parents began coming and paying money into the muffin tin. Trevor gave them change and tickets made out of red construction paper. They sat on folding chairs that Arturo's classmates had put out. Still, there was no Francisco.

The game started out slowly with one walk and one strikeout. LeDru knocked the ball clear into the outfield. Angel caught it but dropped it, and the *Estrellas* got the first home run.

Arturo took a walk. When Trevor was swinging and striking-out, he stole two more bases and then made it home. It was looking good for the *Estrellas*. By the end of the inning, they had two runs.

When the *Lunas* came up to bat, Clorissa lived up to her promise. She slugged the first pitch like a pro and ran past second base before Arturo could pick up the ball and shoot it to third base. She was loping toward third when she saw the ball in front of her and backpedaled quickly to second.

"Yea, *Chorizo*," someone yelled. Everyone laughed at the thought of Clorissa as a spicy Mexican sausage. She certainly wasn't Mexican.

"*Choriza!*" Clorissa yelled back. "That's the feminine."

What a girl, Arturo thought. She could do anything. Arturo shook his head and punched a fist into his mitt. The

Estrellas needed to get moving faster in order to beat the *Lunas*.

The crowd—there were about fifty people or more—really cheered.

Trevor turned out to be a better pitcher than a hitter and struck-out Angel. Angel wasn't doing well as a hitter or as a fielder. Someone yelled for Trevor, "Yea, *Blanco!*"

The innings sailed by rapidly and the score stayed close. The crowd was lively. They yelled for their son's or their daughter's side.

After the next inning, Mr. Moreno let Angel pitch. At last he started doing something right. Wow, could he pitch, thought Arturo, looking at him with surprise. His team started yelling "Go, Valenzuela, go!" Angel turned his cap backward, started strutting on the mound, and spat on the ground like a big-time ball player. The audience laughed as they watched him.

At the bottom of the ninth inning, the score was *Estrellas*, five, *Lunas*, six. The *Estrellas* came up to bat. Earlier, LeDru had hit two homers for the *Estrellas*, and Clorissa had hit one for the *Lunas*. Arturo had barely made it home to give the *Estrellas* their fifth point.

Angel's pitching turned out to be surprisingly skillful. He struck-out *Estrellas* right and left. The close score made Arturo breathe short and quick. He was so tensed and ready to hit a fast one, even though he wasn't up to bat, that he kept moving his shoulders and arms around nervously. The sun was setting. One of the *Lunas* yelled, "Put in Juanita. She hasn't played."

Juanita called back from the baked-goods table. "That's all right!"

"Everyone has to have a turn!" another *Luna* yelled. "We agreed."

So Miss Fenwick put Juanita in, and Arturo and all the *Estrellas* groaned.

Juanita came up to home plate and picked up the bat. It was almost as tall and big around as she was.

She swung wildly at the first ball Angel put over the plate, right at waist level. Arturo cringed and closed his eyes. She missed. The weight of the bat whirled her around. She almost lost her balance. She tried again and missed. Again, there were groans. Someone on the sidelines laughed. Juanita looked like she was about to cry, but she stepped up to the plate and took a firm stand for the third ball. When it came, she swung the bat with a kind of downward chopping motion. Her glasses flew off, her pigtail whirled in the air, and the weight of the bat pulled her off balance. She sat down hard on the ground. The *Estrellas* had lost to the *Lunas*, five to six.

There were groans on one side and cheers on the other.

Juanita sat for a minute, looking dizzy, then got up and picked up her glasses. Her lip quivered. She walked to the muffin tin at the table and began putting money into a coffee can, sniffing as she worked. Arturo was uncomfortable seeing her unhappy. "Hey, Juanita," he said, speaking quietly. "I just wanted to tell you that you are really great at arithmetic!"

She reached out to punch him on the arm, then began laughing. Arturo liked the sound of her laugh.

"I'll help count the money," said Maria. While other kids took in the chairs and the other table, Maria and Juanita counted the money—quarters, dimes, nickels, and dollar bills. After Arturo put the last chair away, he rushed back to the money table to count the stack of dollar bills. There was a lot! When he looked up, he saw the Cruiser parked across the street with three guys next to it. One of them was Francisco. A fine time to arrive, he thought. Arturo started toward his brother. "Hey, Francisco!" he called.

Francisco waved, but the other two got into the car. One opened the back door for Francisco and pulled him in. Then they drove off with that deep, purring sound. Boy, Arturo thought. Talk about goofy or rude or something. Why didn't Francisco at least come over?

Other kids started gathering around. "How did we do?" LeDru was grinning as though he were on top of the world. Even if his team hadn't won, he knew that he was highest-scoring player for the game.

"We made $127.25." Maria's eyes sparkled brightly.

The group was silent for a couple moments. "With what we already have, that makes $891.40," Juanita said, not sounding too happy.

"We need ten thousand dollars in three months. We don't have even a tenth of a down payment on the lot," Clorissa said sadly.

"You finally agree that you are crazy?" Angel had returned to his cool, negative self.

This time no one said anything to disagree.

CHAPTER 13

"CLASS," Miss Fenwick said on Monday morning. "I had a very interesting phone call from a Mr. and Mrs. Chesterton. They read the article about our park project in the newspaper. Mr. Chesterton is a businessman in real estate and said he might be able to help us. When his wife invited me and Mr. Moreno over to talk about it, I said I'd like to bring one of you students because it is your project. So I would like you to choose a class representative."

"I think Arturo should go." Juanita looked at him with a shy smile. "He made the best design for the park."

Everybody thought that was a good idea, and twenty-nine kids voted for Arturo. "I guess you're our duly elected representative," said Mr. Moreno.

Arturo was amazed. He'd never been anybody special before. He was so happy and confused that he closed his eyes for a minute to get his balance. "I . . . I . . . don't know," he stammered. Then he remembered that he hadn't thought he could talk to a reporter, either, but he had. So he gulped and said, "I'll try my best. Thank you."

On the next Saturday, Arturo, in his new red tee shirt that he bought with some of the money Francisco had given him, waited in the school yard where Mr. Moreno and Miss Fenwick picked him up. They drove to the Chestertons' in Miss Fenwick's car.

When they parked in front of the Chestertons' big, beautiful home, Arturo stared. Boy! Did it ever have pretty trees and flowers. The house was almost as big as his apartment building, and the roof rose up in points in a lot of places. Some of the walls were stone and some were made of plaster. As they walked up the slate walk to the carved wooden door under the big, old sycamore trees, Arturo looked up to Mr. Moreno and said, "Wow! This is like a really neat park." The flowers along the walk were bright—pink and lavender and purple and yellow, like those bows Maria was always getting from Buy-Rite.

A small, pretty woman met them at the door. "I'm Jennifer Chesterton," she said. "You must be from Southwood School. Please come in." She led them into the living room where they sat down on a large, flowered couch behind a big coffee table. Arturo couldn't help looking around with wonder at the beautiful room.

A few moments later, Mr. Chesterton strode in. He was a tall, older man with white hair, a rosy complexion, and a happy, successful look. He held out his hand to Arturo. "I'm Elliot Chesterton. What's your name, young man?"

Arturo swallowed nervously and very quietly told him his name as he shook his hand.

Mrs. Chesterton then asked, "Would you like some cookies and milk, Arturo?" When he answered, "Sure!" she left the room. Soon she was back carrying a tray with a coffee server as well as milk and cookies.

As soon as she put the tray on the table, Mr. Moreno took a cookie and started munching.

"Jennifer brought the article in the newspaper about your class to my attention," Mr. Chesterton said, putting on his glasses. "Class with Lots on Its Mind," he read.

"I was surprised when I read where your school was located. The article says that it is bounded by Millard Street to the south, Madison Boulevard on the north, Fidelio Street to the east, and Roosevelt Street to the west.

"That's near the university, not far from my office. I can see why the children don't have any place to play. It's kind of a tough area," he said. "I don't recall seeing a blade of grass or a tree there."

Mrs. Chesterton smiled at her husband. "We were both so touched by the picture of those determined young people," she said. "After reading the article, Elliot's face just lit up, and he said, 'I like their spirit, Jennifer. I'd like to know more about this idea.'"

Mr. Chesterton spoke up briskly. "But that's a mighty big hunk you've bitten off to chew." Then, looking at Mr. Moreno munching his second cookie, he laughed, "I mean the park project, of course."

Arturo smiled a little. He took another cookie, too.

Everyone began talking eagerly. Mr. Moreno sat stiffly upright on the edge of the couch, bouncing his foot, but Miss Fenwick listened quietly to Mr. Chesterton with her eyes focused intently on his face. Arturo watched and listened.

"So, you have an option on the lot that allows you three more months to raise money for a down payment?" Mr. Chesterton asked.

Mr. Moreno brushed cookie crumbs from his mouth. "That's right."

"And you say the total price is fifty-nine thousand? That's a lot of money. How can the class make payments? Where will you get the rest of the money?" Arturo could tell that Mr. Chesterton really understood these things.

"As I frequently say to my students, that's a very good

question." Miss Fenwick looked at Mr. Moreno as if she'd like to know, too. So did Arturo. Such big numbers!

"I guess we figured that we'd take one step at a time. Maybe the Park Department would take the project over after we got it started," Miss Fenwick said.

"Wouldn't it make more sense to buy the land outright?" Mr. Chesterton asked, looking at them earnestly.

What a funny question, thought Arturo. How could they buy the whole thing if they couldn't raise even enough for a down payment?

"That would take magic!" Arturo said and suddenly felt nervous when everyone turned to look at him. Miss Fenwick seemed surprised and pleased with his remark.

"I don't think I believe in magic," Mr. Chesterton said, "but hard work and imagination are almost as good. You and your class seem to have a wealth of those assets." His brow creased as though he were trying to solve a problem. Looking directly at them, he said, "Perhaps we can have a lunch at the Los Angeles City Commerce Club where I'm a member. I could invite some business acquaintances to hear about your project."

Mr. Moreno and Miss Fenwick turned to each other and smiled. "That would be very generous," said Miss Fenwick.

"I'll be happy to arrange a lunch and invite the people, but you and the class have to sell the idea to them," Mr. Chesterton said. He looked at Arturo as if doing so were his responsibility.

Arturo felt important but scared.

"What do you think, Arturo?" Miss Fenwick asked. "Do you think the class would like that?"

Arturo nodded his head up and down.

"Those kids have worked so hard!" Miss Fenwick said. "I'm amazed at their determination. We'll talk to them and take a vote, but I don't think there's any doubt about their decision."

As they were leaving and Mr. Chesterton was telling Miss Fenwick and Mr. Moreno that he'd be happy to help them with advice, Arturo walked over to the window to look into the backyard. Mrs. Chesterton came over to him and said, "Arturo, let's you and I go out and walk around the yard for a few minutes."

Arturo followed her around the lawn, looking at the tennis court, the green bushes, and the tall trees that made a shady canopy over the stone-paved patio, set with a table and chairs. There was even a little waterfall that ran over rocks intermingled with ferns and flowers. Arturo didn't say a word; he was too busy looking. "It's a pretty place, isn't it, Arturo? My husband and I both feel very fortunate that his business success has enabled us to have such a nice yard."

Finally, coming out of his trance while gazing at the blue blossoming water lilies in the fountain, Arturo said, "This is really special."

"Our boys enjoyed it a lot when they were growing up," Mrs. Chesterton said.

Arturo saw a basketball backboard and net on the garage over the driveway.

"Now our grandchildren come and play in it. I think every child should have at least some trees and grass and a place to play."

Arturo turned and smiled at her. What a nice lady, he thought.

When they went back into the house, Mr. Chesterton was saying to the teachers, "Your kids have done a great job.

What they said—their words in that article—sold me on trying to help them. They can do a far better selling job than I can. Jennifer and I will invite thirty-five business people, one for each child. I think it would be helpful if each child wrote a short letter to the person he or she chooses as a guest, and we will enclose it with the invitation."

Mr. Chesterton turned to Arturo, who had just come in. "Would you come with me, Arturo, to talk with the chef at the club about the lunch? We could consult with him right now. I'll give you a ride back to your school."

Arturo looked at his teachers questioningly, and when they smiled approval, he responded with a confident, "Sure!"

The chef at Mr. Chesterton's club suggested a lunch of chicken, rice, vegetables, and salad for the grown-ups and hamburgers for the children.

"How does that sound to you, Arturo?"

"That's fine."

"When my boys were kids, they always ordered hamburgers, even at really nice restaurants. Maybe that's all right." Mr. Chesterton looked thoughtful. But as he got up to leave, he suddenly stopped. "You know, René, if I were a child, I don't think I'd like to sit at a table with a hamburger on my plate and look across the table at a grown-up with a much fancier plate of food. We should all eat the same thing, either chicken or hamburgers. Which would you rather have, Arturo?"

"Hamburgers!" Arturo said emphatically without any hesitation.

"Very good!" said René. "I'll make the best hamburgers in the world for your friends. I will serve them on freshly baked buns we make ourselves along with fruit cocktail and chocolate sundaes for dessert."

Arturo's eyebrows shot up in delight.

Mr. Chesterton reached out and put a firm hand on Arturo's shoulder. They both looked at each other and smiled broadly. "Now we're talking," said Mr. Chesterton.

CHAPTER 14

WHEN MISS FENWICK came into class the next Monday morning, her face was as pink as Juanita's hair ribbon, and her eyes danced with energy that she seemed to be having trouble holding in. Arturo squirmed eagerly because he knew what she was going to say.

"Class, I have something great to tell you. The Chestertons would like to give a fund-raising luncheon for us at the City Commerce Club."

"Ooooh!" "Wow!" said the kids.

"When?" Juanita squeaked. "We don't have much time before the option expires."

Clorissa didn't say a word. She wasn't even looking up, Arturo noticed. Her short, thick braid stuck out behind her head like a curved teapot handle while she read a book. Arturo thought it was strange that she wasn't taking part.

"The luncheon would be in two weeks." Miss Fenwick said. "Yes, Juanita, if we can't come up with the down payment by March, our option will expire and we may have to give up the project. We have less than three months left."

"No! We can't do that!" LeDru sounded fierce.

"But!" Miss Fenwick said dramatically, holding up her forefinger.

"Yeah, there's always a big but!" Arturo commented to a chorus of laughs.

"The 'big but!' as Arturo says, is that there is no way

of knowing how much money people will give at this luncheon. They aren't promising anything. The Chestertons are inviting business people they know, but we have to do the selling. First you each have to write an invitation to the person who will be your guest."

"How do we do that?"

"Let's start by composing one." Miss Fenwick divided the students into small groups, and each group wrote a sample letter, which the class discussed.

"I want each of you to write a letter. You can use ideas from any of the samples or make up your own. I'll mail the letters tonight." Miss Fenwick showed them how they should insert a piece of paper and an envelope for the guest to use to answer the invitation.

After Arturo finished his letter, he felt pleased. This wasn't just a class assignment, he thought. The letter was going to a real person and might help bring them closer to having a park.

"Okay, that part was easy," said Miss Fenwick when the letters had been completed.

"Now let's talk about the hard part," Trevor asked. "How do we sell them our idea?"

LeDru raised his hand. "We can show them pictures of the place as it is now. Then Arturo can show his design of how the place could look."

"Good suggestions," Miss Fenwick said, glancing at Clorissa. She usually had her hand up first thing. "How do you think we could sell this idea, Clorissa? You are awfully quiet today."

"Yes, uh-huh. I suppose we could show them the things we've done. I don't care." She looked back down at her desk and began doodling with her pencil.

Everyone in the class looked around, puzzled. Even Miss Fenwick seemed bewildered.

Something was wrong, Arturo thought. Clorissa cared about everything. She had strong ideas and opinions. She was always full of fine words as if she were giving a speech. Even Angel frowned at her. Arturo felt that they had lost their leader. Oh, sure, Miss Fenwick was their leader, but that was different. She wasn't a kid.

Juanita got back to the subject. "We could give talks at the lunch, tell them what we'd like to do and stuff." She was trying hard. "Clorissa is a good talker. I'll bet she could talk to them."

"Yes, she is," Miss Fenwick agreed. "But we should all say something, each and every one of us."

Maria and Angel looked scared. LeDru looked surprised. Arturo swallowed hard. He couldn't imagine himself standing in front of a room full of grown-up business people, giving a talk to them. "I . . . I'd be too scared and couldn't talk." He could hardly speak just thinking about it. Everyone looked up for Miss Fenwick's reply, as if Arturo had spoken for them, too.

Miss Fenwick didn't seem impressed with Arturo's shyness. "We'll see how it goes a step at a time, Arturo. We can all do more than we think we can. Mr. Chesterton wanted each student to sit alone with his or her guest and talk about our plans."

"What would I say?" Maria burst out. She sounded terrified.

"Good question, Maria. Let's look for the answer to that question. Each of you can take turns being the business person. What kind of questions would you ask if you were the guest? What kind of answers would you give?"

After she divided the class into groups, Miss Fenwick sat down with Angel, LeDru, Arturo, Juanita, Trevor, and Clorissa. Clorissa still hadn't said anything.

"Let's start, LeDru. You be the businessman, Angel."

Having Angel pretend to be a businessman made the group laugh. Angel wrinkled his nose and made a face. "I don't know."

"Okay, Angel, LeDru wants money from you to build a park. What do you want to know before you contribute?"

Angel leaned back in his chair. He half-closed his eyes, and a mischievous smile danced over his lips. He seemed to be having fun pretending he had a lot of money. "Why should I give my money to a bunch of kids?" he asked LeDru. "I would rather buy myself a new Chevy. I'd get a dark red one with Cragar wheels. What would you do with the money if I gave it to you?"

Arturo said, "You make a good businessman, Angel. You're stingy."

"Hey, man, I mean, little boy," Angel snapped. "I'm not going to give you any money if you talk like that."

LeDru looked bewildered.

"Actually, Arturo, Angel's question is exactly the kind that a business person would ask. What else might he ask, Angel?"

"Why do you want to make a park here, little boy?" Angel said to LeDru. The group roared with laughter at Angel calling LeDru "little boy." Angel looked around with pleasure at his audience's response and went on. "You are going to leave this school next year."

Miss Fenwick looked at Clorissa, whose head was still downcast.

LeDru said, "Because there isn't any place for kids to

play in our neighborhood. They play in the street, and you might hit one of us someday when you're driving by. Then we'd sue the pants off you." LeDru burst into laughter and rocked back and forth, stomping the floor with his big feet.

"That's not nice! That would make me mad if I was a business person," Juanita said, frowning and furious. "You should give money to help little children because it's a nice thing to do and will make you feel good. You can help little children like your own. Then they can get exercise and . . . and play hopscotch and jump rope and make little roads and mountains in nice clean sand where it's safe and . . ." Juanita had to stop to take a gulp of air.

At last Clorissa lifted her head. Her big, beautiful dark eyes weren't looking at anyone. She seemed to be gazing out into space at something only she could see.

"Give us help so that we can improve the quality of life for children in our neighborhood. Maybe they will help others when they are grown-up, and . . ." Suddenly Clorissa started crying. She put the back of her hand up to her eyes and wiped the tears away. "Miss Fenwick, may I be excused? I don't feel very well."

"Of course, Clorissa. I'll walk you down to the nurse." Clorissa and Miss Fenwick got up and left.

"What's wrong with Clorissa?" Arturo asked Trevor when Clorissa and Miss Fenwick had left. Her response worried him. Clorissa was so smart and sure of herself. It kind of frightened Arturo that she would cry; he had thought that they could always depend on Clorissa.

When Miss Fenwick came back, several people spoke up. "What's the matter with Clorissa?"

"If Clorissa wants to tell you, she'll do it," said Miss Fenwick, and she sat down with another group.

CHAPTER 15

EVERY DAY Arturo's stomach got more and more nervous. He thought about the lunch meeting coming closer and closer. Could it be true that he was going to talk to a roomful of business people?

"They are just people, like your mothers and fathers and teachers and neighbors. There is no need to be nervous," Miss Fenwick kept saying. "They know you are children. They don't expect you to sound like actors."

Her words helped a little, but not much. Arturo kept busy making a model of the park that would fit into a case Mr. Moreno had brought them. The models of the swings were tricky because they came unglued when the park design was carried in the case. He packed cotton over the swings to keep them from jiggling.

On Wednesday Trevor brought his dad's video camera. He, LeDru, and Arturo took pictures of the lot. Arturo borrowed a couple of the younger Lopez kids, who were sitting on the front steps of their apartment building, and videotaped them playing in the wrecked cars.

But the thought of giving a speech continued to worry Arturo—that, and needing new shoes. His tennis shoes were falling apart.

"Mama, could I have some new shoes?" he asked when she came home from work that day. "The lunch is a week from Saturday."

"I know, *mijo.*" Mama smiled and pinched his cheek, then stood back and looked at him. "You are getting so sturdy and handsome, my little Arturo. To think that you will be speaking to a whole roomful of business people, my little Arturo."

Arturo groaned at the thought.

Mama pinched him on the waist. "And look! My little frog is not so plump anymore. You are stretching up like your uncle." She took his chin in her hand and turned his head sideways. "And look at that nose. It isn't a little pudgy baby nose anymore. It's like the nose of an Aztec warrior on one of those old stone carvings. Papa's people have that nose."

Arturo squirmed and pulled his head away, saying, "Mama, that's enough," though he liked the part about the Aztec warrior. He walked into the bathroom and looked at himself in the mirror. Mama was right; his nose was starting to have a slight arch in it. He returned to his mother in the kitchen. "Mama, what about the shoes?"

"I think we can get some for you, *hijo*, if I get my pay-check in time. I want my son to look good. But my boss is out of town, and I have to wait until he comes back for him to sign the checks."

She squeezed Arturo so hard that his cheek flattened against her. "Now, if I only knew how Francisco was, too."

Mama was still upset about Francisco's leaving. Arturo wasn't worried about him, but he hated to see her unhappy. "Mama, he is with his friends. They are all sworn to protect and . . ."

But Mama was crying again, so Arturo hugged her. Francisco was fine and making lots of money, Arturo felt certain. He would talk to Lobo about letting him join the *Vatos*, too—right after school let out for the summer.

Since Mr. Chesterton had offered to help with the park,

Mama and Papa had stopped saying the teachers and the class were crazy. It was nice to have them be proud of him. Even so, how could he talk in front of all those people?

The next morning in school shortly after the first bell, a messenger came from the office with a letter for LeDru. He looked puzzled as he opened it, but he read the letter quickly, then held it up and waved it excitedly. "Look, everybody! I got an answer to my invitation!" he said, grinning wildly.

Class hadn't started yet, so everyone gathered around LeDru to look at the letter. "Why not wait till everyone is here and then read it to us, LeDru," said Miss Fenwick.

Arturo was fidgety and impatient. Trevor looked at his watch. "It's eight o'clock! If people are late, that's just tough!"

When three more kids had scooted in and sat down, Miss Fenwick said, "You can read it now, LeDru."

LeDru stood rocking back and forth on his big feet as if he were getting ready to make a free throw.

"It starts out," he said and cleared his throat elaborately for comic effect. "Ahem! 'Dear LeDru. Thank you for the invitation to the luncheon. I am pleased to accept and look forward to meeting you and talking with you about your park project a week from Saturday. Sincerely yours, Herbert Donovan.' How about that!" LeDru said. He made a big, sweeping bow and sat down. LeDru never seemed shy, Arturo thought.

"Yea, yea!" Everyone erupted into yells and chattering. "I wonder when mine is coming!" Juanita bounced in her seat. Maria's eyes danced.

Angel came in late and looked around curiously. "What's going on?" he asked.

"If you hadn't been tardy, you'd know, Angel. Ask LeDru during recess. We have to get to work," Juanita said primly.

Once the replies started coming, they poured in. Clorissa, Trevor, and Juanita got theirs on Monday. A flood of letters came on Tuesday, including Maria's and Angel's. During recess Angel strutted around and read the letter to kids from other classes.

"That's not nice," called Juanita while Arturo looked on quietly. He was one of three kids who hadn't received an answer yet. Maybe the person he invited had decided he didn't want to come. Maybe his letter had gotten lost.

He kept practicing his speech anyway. At night he practiced on Mama and Papa. If only Francisco could hear him. He was lonesome without Francisco. He didn't actually worry about him because Francisco was with his close buddies—his *compañeros*. But Mama and Papa were still very worried. Sometimes he would hear the slight clicking of Mama's rosary and her low voice in the bedroom praying Hail Marys, and he knew they were for Francisco.

At school Arturo and his classmates prepared what they would say to their guests. He finished painting his model and helped draw on a roll of white paper a big mural of children playing in a park.

But his shoes. Would there be time to get new ones? Arturo felt kind of dazed by all these things to worry about—and with no reply to his invitation.

Wednesday morning Arturo hurried off to school before Maria could catch him and tag along after him. Across the street from the school, he saw Francisco walking toward him. The Midnight Cruiser was parked there with three *Vatos* in it.

"Francisco!" Arturo called, running to him. "Are you going to go see Mama today?"

Francisco looked thinner and more serious than Arturo remembered him. "No, *chico*. I have just a couple minutes." Francisco glanced back at the guys in the Cruiser, who were watching him.

Arturo couldn't believe that Francisco wouldn't make a quick stop. "Mama has been going to work late this week because she has a cold. She worries about you so much! Go see her."

"I know, but I don't have time. Just tell her I'm . . . I'm all right, and give this money to her and Papa. I miss you all." Francisco ruffled Arturo's hair, handed him a fifty-dollar bill, then trotted back across the street.

"Hey, Francisco!" Arturo gasped when he looked at the numbers on the bill. "Hey, come to visit us. Papa isn't so mad anymore." But the Cruiser, with Francisco between two guys in the backseat, was pulling away from the curb. He looked like a prisoner in the backseat of a police car. Was something funny going on, or was Francisco just busy with his buddies? Arturo looked at the fifty-dollar bill again. He'd never seen so much money! Francisco had to be doing fine. He folded the bill carefully and put it into his shoe. He was nervous even carrying it around.

That day the only other two kids without replies got their letters, leaving Arturo as the only one who had received no response. He had been rejected. There wouldn't be a lunch or any speech for him. All he could think about on the way home was why the letter hadn't come.

When Mama got home from her job, she wasn't smiling. "The boss is still out of town, Arturo. I didn't get my check." She seemed really tired.

Suddenly Arturo remembered the money Francisco had given him and pulled it from his shoe. How could he have forgotten it for a moment? He gave it to Mama and told her about Francisco.

"He's a good boy, my Francisco!" Her face lit up. "He is very busy, but look how generous he is. God has answered my prayers. He is safe and happy. That is all I need."

Something disturbed Arturo when he heard Mama say that Francisco was happy. Was he? He hadn't seemed happy. Maybe he was tired from staying up late or working or partying.

Mama and Arturo caught the bus to Buy-Rite, and he got a super-cool pair of black-and-white running shoes. Mama even bought him a short-sleeved white shirt with buttons down the front—not a tee shirt. "That looks more dressed up," she said, holding it against his shoulders. The shirt looked like something to wear in front of a bunch of grown-ups at an important lunch in a fancy place. A little nervous chill came over him just thinking about it. Arturo put on the shirt and looked at himself in the mirror. He looked old enough for *Los Vatos Locos,* old enough to drive a car, maybe even old enough to take a girl to a movie—maybe Juanita. He laughed with pleasure.

"Do you think Juanita would go to the movies with me?"

"Who?" Mama looked worried.

"Oh, nothing, Mama. It was just a joke."

"It better be!" Mama said, frowning.

The next day was Thursday and Arturo was really worried.

The mail was always delivered to their classroom in the morning, and by noon he still hadn't received a letter. Arturo was miserable. He didn't want to act like a whiny little kid in front of Miss Fenwick. Besides, what could she do if his guest didn't want to come? Thinking of being at home while his whole class went to the lunch made him feel shivery and unhappy.

That night he had dreams about going to the lunch without a guest, sitting all alone and not being asked to show his model or talk about his design. Then the dream changed. Suddenly he was in front of a lot of men in business suits. He forgot what he was supposed to say, and they scowled at him. "Send him home! Send him home!" they began to chant. "We didn't want him anyway. That's why we didn't answer his invitation." Hot and sweaty, he tossed and turned and hardly slept at all.

CHAPTER 16

ON FRIDAY MORNING Arturo felt rotten. He had no appetite, and he was unhappy and droopy from lack of sleep. He knew he was going to be embarrassed in front of the whole class. Maybe he should play hooky and skip the whole school day.

But he dressed automatically, drank a glass of milk, and grabbed a stale *pan dulce*. Munching the sweet roll, he started slowly down the stairs. How could he face being the only one without a guest at tomorrow's lunch? Arturo walked slowly, looking at the sidewalk. He felt really lousy. Maybe he was getting the flu. Then he heard Maria's voice right behind him.

"*Hola*, Arturo. Are you excited about the lunch tomorrow? I got a new blouse!" Maria was skipping and flouncing around happily. "Did you get anything new?"

"Yeah, I got a shirt and shoes."

"Wow, it's going to be so neat."

Arturo was angry. He set his jaw tightly and clamped his teeth together. It wasn't fair. Why hadn't his guest answered?

When they got to school, Arturo was still angry. Miss Fenwick and Mr. Moreno always said you should speak up when you have a problem, but Papa said speaking up just got you into trouble. Arturo stood in the hall, their words whirling around inside him. He really wanted to know. . . . He felt so bad about not getting an answer to his invitation that he decided to speak up. He took a deep breath and walked into the school office.

"I'm Arturo Morales," he said to the woman behind the desk. "I'm in Miss Fenwick's class. You know how all the kids in our class have been getting letters? Did a letter come for me?"

The woman turned and spoke to a girl who looked as if she were still in high school. "Felicia, are there any more letters for Miss Fenwick's class?"

"No, there weren't any letters for her class in yesterday's or today's mail." Felicia looked at Arturo. "I've delivered them all, unless a few came before Joellen quit that she didn't give to me to distribute."

"Joellen? Oh, yes. Where did she keep them?"

"I don't know. She never mentioned it."

Arturo stood on tiptoes to see behind the counter. "It's awfully important. Could you look, please?"

Felicia rummaged under the counter and brought out a box full of mail. "No, this is the teachers' box." She turned back to Arturo. "I'm afraid I don't see anything."

Arturo walked out the door and down the hall. If a person couldn't come, you'd think he would at least tell you so you could invite someone else, he thought with annoyance. He wanted to go right home so he wouldn't have to face his classmates, but his legs, heavy as hunks of concrete, kept moving toward his classroom.

Then he heard someone walking rapidly toward him, almost running. It was Felicia, and she was holding an envelope. "What did you say your name was?" she asked.

"Arturo Morales."

She beamed broadly at him. "Here's your letter. It's been sitting in Miss Fenwick's file for a couple of weeks. It didn't dawn on me that Joellen might have kept them there." Felicia held out the letter.

"Thank you!" Arturo said, and he looked at the letter as if it were magic. He was almost afraid to open it. The return address said Countrywide Life Insurance Company. Maybe, after all this waiting, he would get a refusal. He tore the envelope open and read the letter quickly. His guest was coming. He was coming! "I would be very happy to attend your luncheon," the letter said. The words of the reply, almost the same as those the other kids had received, seemed so different, so much more real. The letter made him feel important and special. It was signed, "Steven Khourian." Arturo took a deep breath and laughed, feeling himself expand until he was as light as a balloon.

When Miss Fenwick asked if anyone hadn't received an answer, not a hand went up. Then she asked, "How many guests couldn't come?"

"Mine couldn't," said Maria, "but another lady sent a note, and Mr. Chesterton said she could come instead."

"So everyone has a guest." Miss Fenwick said, applauding joyfully. "We've done a lot of work getting ready for the lunch. Tomorrow let's relax and have fun."

Relax! Arturo was suddenly hit with the realization that he had a presentation to give with his model. For a few minutes, he'd forgotten about it.

Saturday, the day of the lunch, Arturo put on his black pants, his new white shirt, and his cool-looking athletic shoes. After combing his newly cut straight black hair again and again, he finally got it to lay down smooth and neat, even the part in back that usually stuck up. Lifting the case holding his model, which Miss Fenwick had let him take home to show to Mama and Papa, he walked carefully to school. His stomach felt as if it were going down a slide, then up on a swing. The strange faces staring at him in his dream popped back into his mind. The lunch guests would expect something smart. Would he forget his speech? The thought of it made his stomach do a high dive.

Mr. Chesterton sent a bus to the school yard to pick up the whole class and the teachers. When Arturo arrived, almost half the kids were there already. Angel had on a new shirt with a pink stripe. His curls were combed back all shiny with some hair goop that smelled really strong.

The bus came right on time. Everyone was very quiet as they drove to the club. Maybe they were nervous, too, Arturo thought. The bus drove right up to the front of a big hotel-like building in the middle of town. A green cloth canopy over the entrance said, "City Commerce Club." The place sure looked elegant.

They were a little early, but they were shown right into the dining room. Arturo helped Trevor and LeDru to tape up the mural behind the platform. Then he opened the case and laid his model of the park on a table so that people would pass it coming in. It made Arturo feel all tingly to see the model sitting there so importantly in such a nice place. The swings hadn't come unglued, the flowers made of red and orange beads were still in place. Just looking at his model made him expand with pride. Only one corner of green-flocked paper lawn was unstuck, and it curled up a little. He pushed it down, but it wouldn't stick.

Trevor set up the slide projector to show the pictures he and LeDru had taken. Then he plugged in the tape deck. Miss Fenwick checked the microphone and the light on the podium. When everything was set up, they all sat down at their places at the tables. Arturo had looked around the tables and found a card with "Arturo Morales" written on it. He sat down and put his model case by his chair.

To Arturo the room looked like something on a TV program, the tables with their white tablecloths, the fancy glasses and silverware. He imagined giving his talk to people in this place. As Arturo looked around the beautiful room, the colors of the yellow and blue flowers on the white tables started to blur and swim. He knew that all the other kids were there, too, but he hardly paid any attention to them. Besides, most of them didn't have to give a speech as long as his.

Gradually other people came in. There were a lot of men—mostly Anglo—wearing gray suits or blue suits. One man with white hair was wearing a navy blue jacket. Arturo thought it might have been Mr. Chesterton but he was too nervous to really notice. Some people wore sports shirts.

Soon a man with a gray suit and a matching fringe of hair around his bald head came to Arturo's table. After reading the place card in front of Arturo, he held out his hand and said, "I'm Steven Khourian. You must be Arturo. I'm very happy to meet you, Arturo."

"I'm happy to meet you, Mr. Khourian." Arturo stood up and shook his hand, remembering what they practiced in class.

Mr. Khourian had friendly eyes behind his rimless glasses. Arturo thought he looked like somebody's grandfather. Maybe Trevor's grandfather. "Your letter said your business was insurance. What kind of insurance do you sell, Mr. Khourian?" Arturo asked stiffly.

It turned out to be pretty easy to talk to Mr. Khourian.

He asked Arturo questions that weren't even about the park, questions about Arturo's classes and his family. "So, do you want to be a designer?" he asked. "Perhaps a landscape architect?"

Arturo looked surprised. He hadn't thought that he could do something he liked so well as a job.

"Maybe," he heard himself say. A landscape architect. He liked the sound of it.

The waiters, wearing white jackets, were bringing in the food. One put a tall-stemmed glass filled with fruit in front of Arturo. Suddenly he felt nervous again and didn't think he could eat.

Trevor got up to start the music. He looked like a miniature businessman in his light blue jacket, white shirt, tie, and navy blue pants. The tape deck started playing Cat Stevens's "Where Do the Children Play?"

When the song was over, Miss Fenwick spoke to the group. Arturo knew that she was telling the business people about everything the class had done to raise money and how hard they had worked, but he wasn't really listening. His heart pounded faster when he remembered that he would be talking pretty soon. Mr. Moreno spoke for awhile about how he had intended to have the class plan an "ideal city," but it had become clear that working on their own neighborhood would be better. "It could certainly use the work," he said. Both he and Miss Fenwick must have said a lot of good things because people really clapped after each of their talks.

Then Trevor showed his video and some slides of the dump. There were the two little Lopez kids playing in the concrete rubble. Some kids from their class were in the pictures, too. Trevor told the guests about how the class wanted to change what they saw in the video and slides into something better.

When Clorissa got up to walk toward the platform, Arturo was proud that she was the leader of his group. Today Clorissa didn't look like the best slugger on the softball team. She was suddenly a pretty young lady in a bright yellow sundress with a big yellow ribbon on top of her thick, curved braid. Whatever had been bothering her a while ago seemed gone, Arturo thought. She looked quite self-assured.

Arturo pushed back his chair, smiled at Mr. Khourian, walked up front, and stepped up to the podium with Clorissa and the others. Clorissa's clear, confident voice came from behind Arturo, above his head, but he didn't comprehend the words until she said, "This is Arturo Morales, our designer. He made the model of our park. He will now tell you about it."

The faces in front of Arturo blurred, his ears rang, and he couldn't say a word. Suddenly he felt Clorissa's hand squeezing his shoulder. He relaxed a bit, and the words started coming out mechanically. "We want our park to be for little kids, so I tried to remember what it was like to be little. There are a lot of little kids in my apartment building across the street from the dump. So, I thought of what they would like to do and . . ."

Gradually, Arturo relaxed. Everyone was smiling at him in an encouraging way. They sat up straight and listened carefully, as if they thought he were important. At the end of his presentation, he realized that giving a speech hadn't been so bad after all. He smiled broadly and relaxed some more.

At last he could pay attention to the people in the audience. A lady in a blue dress was dabbing at her eyes with a tissue. She must have a cold or an allergy, Arturo thought as he stepped back from the podium and let Juanita have her turn. Juanita must have been on the bus, though Arturo hadn't noticed her until now. She looked really pretty in a ruffly white dress and a headband. She didn't have pigtails today. Her hair hung long and loose with slight curls at the tips.

Juanita said she wanted little children to have a clean place to play, one without broken glass or fish heads. Everyone laughed at the fish heads, even though what she said was true.

Clorissa finished the group's presentation, and Arturo listened carefully as she said, "Building a park would be a great achievement for us. I knew that I would have to put a lot of effort into this project, but that if we succeeded I could look back and say, 'You know, I've done this.' My parents would feel proud, too, and the feeling would go on for generations and generations."

Clorissa's words sounded like a real speech by a grown-up. Her words made Arturo realize again that what they were doing was important. Lots of people were dabbing at their eyes. As Arturo walked back to sit down, Mr. Khourian sniffed loudly, wiped his nose, and put his hanky away. "You did great, son," he said. Arturo couldn't remember when he'd felt so happy.

With a grin, Arturo looked hungrily at his hamburger, which even had avocados and bacon. While he was devouring his burger, the rest of the kids gave their presentations. The kids who spoke English and Spanish translated for the ones who spoke only Spanish.

There was a lot of applause and talking afterward.

Everyone was happy and noisy as they rode back to the

school on the bus. Miss Fenwick and Mr. Moreno led them in songs. Juanita sat down beside Arturo. "You gave a nice talk, Arturo, and everybody liked your model."

"Thanks. I liked your talk about the fish heads." Arturo felt proud. "Mr. Khourian asked if I was going to be a landscape designer." Arturo laughed, like the idea was a joke. He wanted to see what Juanita would say.

"Why not?" she asked. "I might be a bookkeeper, or an accountant—that's even harder!" She sounded excited. Then her tiny voice became serious. "I hope that they give us enough money to build the park."

Arturo realized that he had forgotten about the reason for the luncheon, though Juanita hadn't. She would be a good bookkeeper—or accountant.

Arturo ran most of the way home, eager to tell Mama and Papa about the luncheon. But on La Luna, he saw a police car in front of his apartment building. Arturo froze with fear. Police cars never meant anything good. As Arturo walked up the stairs, a young Anglo policeman with reddish hair walked down carrying a notepad. His face wore a serious expression. Arturo wanted to know what had happened, but he didn't like to speak to policemen, so he kept his eyes down and hurried past the officer. Even before he got to his apartment door, he heard Mama crying, and when he opened the door, Papa was standing there holding Mama in his arms. She was sobbing loudly, "No, no! It isn't true!"

"Come in, *mijo*," Papa said, his voice heavy with sadness. "It's about Francisco. Something terrible has happened."

CHAPTER 17

THE WHOLE LOPEZ FAMILY was in Arturo's apartment with Mama and Papa. Mr. Lopez leaned quietly in the doorway, looking at Arturo's parents. The toddler hung onto her four-year-old sister, and the five year old sat quietly on Papa's green plastic lounger, looking scared.

Mama was crying loudly. "No, no! It isn't true. Not Francisco!" Suddenly she broke away and rushed into the bedroom. "We have to go to the hospital right away! Oh, my poor little Francisco! Let's go right now. Where's my purse?"

"Papa, what happened to Francisco?"

But Papa had gone into the bedroom after Mama.

"What happened?" Arturo was terrified and started after Papa.

Mr. Lopez stopped Arturo by the arm and led him into the hall. "Your brother has been shot, Arturo, but he was not killed. He is in the hospital, and the doctors are working hard to save him."

"But why?" Tears sprang from Arturo's eyes like a shower.

"It must have been the Thirty-thirders," Mr. Lopez said. "Haven't they been fighting with *Los Vatos?* Someone tried to kill him."

"If he dies, I'm going to get one of them, too! I will!" Arturo yelled.

"No, no, don't talk that way, Arturo. Do you want to cause your mother more pain?" Mrs. Lopez touched Arturo's shoulder, but he pushed her away angrily and wiped his eyes.

How had Francisco's buddies let this awful thing happen?

Arturo wondered. *Los Vatos Locos* are strong. He sobbed deeply, then choked out, "They can't do this to my brother. I will get those dirty Thirty-thirders, and you can't stop me! They must have got him when he was alone. His buddies would have protected him. That's what *compas* are for." Arturo was angry at the whole world for letting such a thing happen. He glared at Mr. Lopez angrily, as if he had shot Francisco. His disordered thoughts swam around in his head. He punched the wall with his fist and brought it back in pain. With a new gush of tears, all his strength left him. Mrs. Lopez put her arms around him.

"Why did they do it? Why did they do it?" Arturo asked weakly as he clung to her.

She did not answer but held his head close to her. After a couple of moments, Papa came out into the hall. Arturo stood up straight and wiped his nose. "Let's go, Papa! Right now!"

Papa reached into his pocket and gave Arturo a quarter. "Go quickly to Julio's and call your Aunt Yolanda and Uncle Juan. Tell them to come quickly. We will be faster in their car than on the bus. I'll stay with Mama."

Arturo started down the stairs rapidly, glad to be able to do anything. When he got to Julio's market, he saw Maria and Angel standing on the street corner. Arturo quickly made his call. Uncle Juan said that they would come right away.

Maria looked at Arturo with a solemn expression as he was leaving. "Arturo, I heard about Francisco. I hope he will be all right. It is a terrible thing," Maria said.

Angel, usually so cool and tough, looked pale and frightened. "Hey, man, Francisco was a real cool dude. It's too bad."

His words woke Arturo up. "Don't say *was*. He's not dead." Looking at Angel, he thought of Angel's cousin, *El Lobo*. "Do you know who did it, or does your cousin?"

"Why would I know, man?" Angel seemed flustered. "I don't know. I haven't talked to my cousin for a long time."

"Doesn't he know what's going on? Are the *Vatos* going to get the dirty Thirty-thirder who shot Francisco?"

Angel lifted his shoulders and held out his hands. "Hey, man, I don't know."

Aunt Yolanda and Uncle Juan came quickly and drove Arturo and his parents to the hospital. The nurse broke the hospital rules and let Arturo go into the intensive-care ward, even though he was under fourteen. Francisco was sedated and lay sleeping in the white hospital bed. His ghostly pale skin made him look dead.

The room was so quiet you could hear the tiny hissing sound of oxygen coming out of the tube under Francisco's nose. The bed was so high that Mama couldn't look into his face, so the nurse got a stool for her. Mama climbed up and kissed Francisco, then began sobbing, *"Mijo, Panchito,"* calling him by his pet name.

Papa stood behind her, looking sad and helpless.

Tears prickled Arturo's nose, and he sniffed loudly. The nurse said that they should let Francisco rest, so Papa led them out. The doctor talked to them in the hall and said that Francisco had been shot in the chest, that a lung had collapsed, and that he had lost a lot of blood. They would do the best they could for him, he said, then he nodded and walked away.

"Papa," asked Arturo, "will the police find who shot him?"

"They said they will try, *hijo,* but I don't think they will succeed."

When Arturo got to school late on Monday morning, he didn't care much about anything. But today Miss Fenwick seemed to be shining all over. Even her blonde hair sparkled with slight golden glints.

"The luncheon was a big success," she said. "Mr. Chesterton called me to say that the guests had pledged THIRTY THOUSAND DOLLARS!"

"Thirty thousand dollars?" Mr. Moreno and the class gasped in unison. Arturo's jaw dropped in surprise.

Everyone else was crazy with happiness. Juanita did her jumping, whirling, and skipping routine. Clorissa talked about "attaining goals." Mr. Moreno rocked back and forth on his sneakers and smiled all over his face. Miss Fenwick, who was usually so serene and cautious, didn't once say, "Now, students, remember that what we are really going to get from all of this is extremely valuable experience and knowledge—no matter how it turns out."

What she did say was, "Later today, Mr. Chesterton is coming to give a report on the details. First let's write some really nice thank-you letters to those wonderful people."

Arturo felt dazed. The picture of Francisco lying in his hospital bed stood between him and the world. He felt cheated. He tried to remember talking about his design and the questions people had asked him about his model. He carefully wrote:

Dear Mr. and Mrs. Chesterton,

I hope you had a good time at the lunch like I did. Everything was wonderful after I got over being scared. The food and the bus and, most important, the money. Thank you very much.

Sincerely,
Arturo Morales

Arturo remembered how happy and excited he had been. How could one part of his life be so wonderful and another so miserable? How could his class be so happy while Francisco might be dying? Anger ate into his stomach. He clenched his jaw tightly and ground his teeth. He had to help the *Vatos* get whoever shot his brother.

CHAPTER 18

"LET'S SEE." Juanita was reading to the class from her treasurer's notebook. "We've got plenty for the down payment, but even with the thirty thousand dollars and the $891.30 in our bank account, we still need $28,108.70." She frowned. "We are going to graduate and leave this school in less than six months. How can we get enough money to make a park by then?"

The entire class was quiet as though discouraged. The park no longer seemed important to Arturo. He was thinking of Francisco.

"We can't act this miserable when Mr. Chesterton comes this afternoon," Clorissa said. "He worked hard for us. We can't let him think we are ungrateful."

No one said anything.

"We'll have to be honest with him," said Miss Fenwick.

When Mr. Chesterton arrived that afternoon, he seemed as happy as a kid at a birthday party. As he sat on a chair in front of the room, Arturo and Trevor exchanged a solemn look of concern that Mr. Chesterton wouldn't be so happy when he left.

"Students," he said, "your hard work on the luncheon really produced results. As you know, people pledged over thirty thousand dollars, and I've had a number of phone calls telling me what a fantastic job you all did. Everyone was tremendously impressed with each and every one of you.

Can you believe that I got calls from people who I didn't even ask to the luncheon who just wanted to give money?" He looked extremely pleased.

Arturo started to tingle all over and couldn't keep from smiling a little. He felt that he was catching whatever emotion Mr. Chesterton had. He saw others start to smile, too.

Thinking about the numbers Juanita had read to them that morning, Arturo remembered how hard he had worked making the model and the intense, focused feeling that work had given him—like playing in a really fast soccer game. The feeling broke through suddenly, and he realized how much he wanted the project to succeed. He wanted to help make that park. But how? It seemed impossible—even after all their work.

Juanita smiled weakly like a little owl behind her big, round glasses. Arturo could see that she wasn't going to say anything to Mr. Chesterton about how much money they still needed. That would be like saying, "Oh, thirty thousand dollars? Hey, man, we can't do anything with that unless we have at least thirty thousand more." No way was she or probably anyone else going to say anything about needing more money.

"But I have more good news to tell you." Mr. Chesterton smiled as though he had a secret. "I talked to an organization called The Los Angeles Community Foundation. Their job is to give away money."

"Wow, are they crazy?" said Angel. "I'd keep my money."

"The Foundation is a philanthropic organization. Do you know what that means?"

"It means charitable," said Trevor. "A group that gives away money to help people."

"Right, Trevor," Mr. Chesterton continued. "I told this

organization about your park project, and they offered us 'matching funds.' Do you know what that means?''

"I can figure that out!" LeDru was grinning wildly.

"Does it mean they might give us . . . ?" Arturo's mouth fell open. He couldn't believe what he was thinking.

"Would they really give us . . ." Clorissa stared intently, "the same amount as . . . ?"

"Yes, they've already pledged thirty thousand dollars more for your park project!" Mr. Chesterton's eyebrows arched, and his face glowed.

The clapping and cheering went on and on. After it stopped, Arturo was surprised to find that he had been clapping and cheering, too.

Miss Fenwick got up and took Trevor's hand in one of hers and Maria's in the other and started dancing around the room. Other kids grabbed on and added to the chain.

Arturo took Juanita's hand with one of his and grasped LeDru's with the other. Mr. Moreno took Clorissa's hand, and she took someone else's. Pretty soon everyone in the class had joined hands and was skipping around Mr. Chesterton, who stood there, his face glowing as red as a stoplight. Arturo could see that he was happy and embarrassed at the same time.

Someone started to chant. "We did it! We did it! We did it!" Nobody said a word about not making so much noise for fear of bothering the other classes.

After they stopped dancing, Arturo felt funny holding Juanita's small hand. She looked at him and smiled shyly. He felt embarrassed and dropped her hand. Then, remembering Francisco, he felt ashamed. How could he be happy when his brother might be dying?

After the class thanked Mr. Chesterton one more time,

he waved good-bye and left. The kids stood around talking excitedly until everyone had to leave to catch their buses. Arturo and Juanita were the last ones in the room. She got a stack of books out of her desk. "After all that," she said, "I don't really feel like doing my homework, but I don't want to fall behind." Then, looking at Arturo, she said, "Aren't you taking home any books? We have a big arithmetic assignment."

"Uh, I . . ."

"You really should."

"Maybe so." He went back and picked up a couple of books without even looking at them.

"Aren't you going to take your arithmetic book?"

"Oh," Arturo said. He wanted to talk to Juanita about Francisco, but he couldn't. "Did you ever find out what Clorissa was upset about?" he asked.

"She was really unhappy because her friend Vanetta— you know, the runner she always talked about—well, she was going to go to college on an athletic scholarship, but, well, she's going to have a baby."

Having a baby didn't seem as important as Francisco's problem. Arturo furrowed his brow to look concerned. "That's a bummer. I mean, since she wanted to go to college."

"Clorissa was real upset for a while because she said Vanetta could have gotten a start into a better life and everything, but now. . . . Well, Clorissa said that what happened to Vanetta certainly wasn't going to happen to her and that she was going to try for a scholarship when she's in high school. She'll get one, too. Clorissa is so smart."

Arturo couldn't hold the words back any longer. "Juanita, my brother, Francisco, got shot on Saturday, the day we had the luncheon, and I . . . I don't feel . . ."

Juanita reached out and took Arturo's hand. "That's terrible, Arturo. I'm so sorry for him—and for your family. Maria told me about it. How did it happen? Why don't you come over to my house, and we can do our arithmetic together. It's better to do something than to just feel bad."

"I am going to do something. I am going to get the guy who shot Francisco. It has to be one of the Thirty-thirders."

"Don't talk like that!" Juanita put her hand to her mouth.

On the way over to Juanita's, Arturo talked to her about Francisco and *Los Vatos*, about how close the guys were. He told her they were sworn to help each other if any of them needed anything. "I'm going to go talk to Lobo," Arturo said. "I want to help them get that dirty . . ."

Juanita listened quietly. Arturo felt better talking to her. "I'm going on the bus this evening to see Francisco at the hospital. Mama won't go to work as long as he is there. She stays with him during the day. Papa will go over after work." Arturo sniffed and rubbed his nose briskly, so Juanita wouldn't know he felt like crying. "He was shot in the chest."

"I bet he'll be all right soon." Juanita's voice was tiny but sounded so certain that Arturo felt she must be right.

They were both silent for a few moments. Then Arturo thought of something that had a little bit to do with arithmetic.

"If it costs us fifty-nine thousand dollars just to buy the land for the park, we won't have any money left to build it with, will we? After all, trees and sidewalks and equipment and stuff cost money too. Can we, I mean, do we?"

Juanita lowered her eyes. "Why don't we just be happy for a while over how much we do have."

CHAPTER 19

EVERY MORNING since Francisco had been shot, Mama walked to St. Augustine's over on Van Buren Street for six o'clock mass. She said her rosary and lit a candle for Francisco before she went to the hospital. Sometimes Mama got Arturo out of bed early and said, "Come to church with me, *mijo*, and say a prayer for your brother." Sometimes Arturo went.

One morning after Arturo and Mama had gone to mass and Arturo was on his way to school, thinking about Francisco and hoping his prayers would help, he saw a police car parked at the curb. He didn't like police. They made him nervous, but there wasn't any other way to find out. He walked over and waved at the officer. When the police-man rolled down the window, Arturo asked, "Have you found out anything about who shot my brother, Francisco Morales?" The officer said that he hadn't, but that he would let Arturo's family know if they learned anything important. Arturo didn't have much hope.

That afternoon when he got home from school, the whole family rode the bus to see Francisco. Four days had passed since the shooting, and Francisco had "stabilized," the doctor said, but was still too weak to talk much.

At school the next day during their park meeting, Trevor asked the same question that Arturo had asked Juanita. "What will we use to build the park after we spend all our money on the land?"

Clorissa sat slumped and dejected. "Mr. Moreno, we are graduating in June. We want to leave a park to the neighborhood children as a legacy. It would be so disappointing if we didn't finish it after coming this far."

Arturo didn't like to see Clorissa discouraged. Today she looked as if she had lost hope. If even Clorissa got discouraged, what could be done? Maybe even someone as strong as Clorissa needed encouragement sometimes. Arturo blurted out, "We are so close! We can't stop now!"

Angel said, "Hey, I've got an idea."

A bunch of kids scowled at him. Nothing Angel said was ever good. LeDru frowned angrily. "Hey, dude, we aren't in no mood for your bad mouth."

"Hey, no, man," Angel said. "This is real. When my cousin Juan wanted to buy a '71 Chevy Monte Carlo, the dude wanted seven hundred and fifty bucks at a hundred dollars a month."

Arturo knew Juan—*El Lobo*—the head of *Los Vatos Locos*. He realized suddenly that Lobo hadn't come over to talk to his family about the shooting.

"So," Angel continued, "my cousin said, 'Hey, no way.'" Angel's narrow-eyed smirk said he had something big to tell. "Juan said, 'Hey, man, I give you four hundred fifty cash.' The guy said, 'Five hundred, man, and you got one hot cruiser.'"

The whole class stared at Angel. Trevor's mouth fell open with amazement. "That's terrific. Let's offer Mrs. Edmonds less than her asking price of fifty-nine thousand dollars, but let's offer her cash. Then we'll have money left to build the park!"

Angel pointed to Trevor. "Pretty smart, *Blanco!* You figure that out by yourself?"

"Good thinking, guys," said Mr. Moreno. "Bargain! Classic real-estate and car-purchasing technique. When Mr. Chesterton arrives, we'll tell him. I'm sure he'll approve." Mr. Moreno gave one of his undefeatable grins. "Dynamite suggestion, gentlemen. Now to negotiate with the owner."

When Mr. Chesterton came that afternoon, he told the class about the laws and rules governing real-estate transactions. About an option, for instance. Arturo couldn't have cared less a few months ago about something called an option. Now he knew that an option meant that Mrs. Edmonds would not sign a contract with another buyer for the time they had agreed upon. She was holding the land for them. He listened as Mr. Chesterton explained that a contract was an agreement between two parties, like people or companies, to transact business. "Once an offer has been accepted and both parties agree to the transaction, then a third party," Mr. Chesterton said, "like a bank or an escrow company, places all of the necessary documents and money into escrow. The escrow officer assures the buyer that the deed correctly describes the property and that both parties' expenses are paid."

Mr. Chesterton then unrolled maps of the land from the county recorder's office. As Arturo looked at them, a feeling of power grew in him. He understood them. "Hey, they are drawn to scale!" He thought, Heck, I'm almost a landscape designer.

"Your land has to be rezoned for use as a park," Mr. Chesterton said, holding the drawings for all to see.

"What's rezoned?" asked Arturo.

Mr. Chesterton told them that the government decides

what kind of buildings will be permitted in any area or "zone."

"Yeah, so someone can't start a pig farm next door to you." LeDru laughed.

"I guess nobody heard about those laws in our barrio," said Angel. "There's already a junkyard next to Arturo's apartment."

"So," Mr. Chesterton continued, "I'll file a request for rezoning. You wouldn't want to buy the land and then find out you couldn't use it for a park, would you?"

There was a loud gasp from the class.

"They wouldn't refuse us, would they?" Juanita asked and bit her lip nervously.

"Why not? The city has refused everything else we've asked for," Angel said with a sneer. "We'd own our very own dump!"

"Does it take long to get permission?" Trevor asked. "We want to finish the park before we graduate in June."

Mr. Chesterton shrugged. "Each case is different. Nothing in life is certain. Government processes are usually pretty slow. We should be sure that the property will be rezoned before we sign a contract to buy it."

"It would be awful if we couldn't get the zoning changed after we've gotten this far." LeDru said.

Arturo spoke up without even thinking about feeling nervous. "Before you got here, Mr. Chesterton, Angel said we should bargain with Mrs. Edmonds to get a lower price for paying her in cash." He hated giving Angel credit for the idea, but it was his.

"An excellent idea," said Mr. Chesterton. "That's very businesslike. Bargaining is definitely the way to go."

Angel's dark curls were hanging onto his forehead, and

his face was tense with eager interest for a change. Imagine him actually paying attention to the project, Arturo thought.

"Class, I have an idea I need your opinion on," Mr. Chesterton said. "I know an architecture student from the university who might be willing to help you draw the plans for the park to submit to the city. Would you like to interview her? She's about to graduate, and working on a real project would help her."

Miss Fenwick had the class discuss the idea and vote. Arturo thought he'd like to meet someone who was really learning to be a designer. Maybe he could learn something from her. Then he remembered Francisco. First he had to find Francisco's attacker.

Maybe, just maybe the park was going to become a reality—trees and bushes and flowers and swings. But he was getting way ahead of the project. They hadn't even bought the land.

After a strongly positive vote, they composed a letter on the blackboard inviting Ms. Caroline Otaro-Schultz to meet the class and discuss the project.

"What about Arturo's plans?" Juanita asked, looking over at him.

He was quiet, wondering if any of his design would be used.

"Arturo and all the rest of you will be the architect's clients," Mr. Chesterton said as he stood up to leave. "That's the way it works when my company plans a project. You will work with her, tell her what you want and what you don't want. Then she will draw up the plans. See you later, kids. If I stay away from my job too long, I might get fired." He raised his eyebrows playfully.

The kids waved and laughed. After all, who could fire the boss? Arturo wondered.

Once Mr. Chesterton had gone, LeDru looked concerned. "I don't know about that lady architect student. Adults are always trying to horn in and take things away from kids."

"We won't let them do that," Clorissa said. She was back in her former positive mode. "But we do need professional help."

"Whatever happens, we will have a wonderful learning experience finding out how these things are really done," Miss Fenwick said for about the fiftieth time, Arturo thought.

"Yeah, sometimes deals fall through in real life, too." Angel's oblique glance looked very cool. Arturo thought of how Francisco had probably been somebody's "deal" that had fallen through. Today he had to talk to Lobo. He wondered if any of the gang had finally gone over to visit Francisco.

When Mr. Moreno left the class that day, he waved and said, "Wish me luck. I'm going to call Mrs. Ethel Edmonds and see if we can change our option!"

"Good luck, Mr. Moreno," Clorissa called. *"Buena suerte,"* Arturo echoed in Spanish, followed by almost thirty voices wishing Mr. Moreno two kinds of luck—English and Spanish.

After school, Arturo spoke to Angel. "Hey, man, where does your cousin hang out? I want to talk to him about helping the *Vatos* find which one of those Thirty-thirders shot Francisco."

Angel looked away from Arturo. "How do I know where my cousin hangs out? He doesn't tell me his business."

Arturo gritted his teeth. Angel was the kind of little punk he could enjoy beating to a pulp. "Well, he is the head of Francisco's *clika*. I thought maybe he could come to our house and tell us what he knows—you know, try to help. Has he gone to see Francisco?"

"Hey, how many times I have to tell you? I don't know nothing, *nada*, about my cousin's business, okay?" Angel strode off, leaving Arturo angrily punching his fist into his palm.

Mama and Papa and Arturo went to the hospital that evening. They pushed the button outside the intensive-care ward, and the nurse let them into the quiet, dim room. Above Francisco's head a monitor showed green lines of light. The lines stretched longer, then shrank to short points in a changing pattern, his brother's life pulsing through the machines.

Francisco opened his eyes halfway. "Mama. Papa." His voice was a thin whistle. Arturo went closer and said, *"Hola, hermano,"* and then squeezed Francisco's arm gently. *"Qué pasa,* man?" he asked softly.

Francisco looked too weak to make loud noises but an expression that was almost a smile came to his lips when he heard Arturo ask him, "What's happening?" in Spanish.

"Has Lobo or any of the guys been to see you?" Arturo asked, looking into Francisco's eyes. There was no flicker of pleasure at the mention of his *compañeros*, but Arturo thought he saw a slight side-to-side motion of his head. Arturo thought it was his imagination; surely Lobo and the others would have come to see him.

"Son," Papa said, "we want you to be well more than anything. Then we will plan a way for you to be safe. Who shot you, my son?"

Francisco's eyes were almost shut. He looked sad—or

was he only sleepy? Arturo waited tensely for his answer. Francisco's mouth barely opened, and he made a weak, breathy sound. It sounded like, "Maybe . . ." Then, breathing heavily, his eyes closed.

"Was it the Thirty-thirders?" Arturo asked, squeezing his brother's arm harder, but it was no use. Francisco was asleep.

"He talked! He talked!" Mama was laughing and tearful at the same time. She pushed his dark hair aside, then climbed on the stool to kiss Francisco on the forehead.

"Come, let him sleep now. Let him get better." Papa had to tear Mama away. "He needs all his strength to get well."

"I am going to stay here tonight," Mama said determinedly. "The nurse will get me a cot like she did yesterday. Francisco needs me." She fidgeted with her purse.

Papa led her out by the arm while she dabbed at her eyes with a tissue.

As they were leaving the room, they met the doctor coming in. He was a dark-haired man with a hooked nose and an accent that wasn't Spanish. He explained that Francisco looked better but still was not ready to leave the intensive-care ward.

Mama and Papa stood quietly, too shy to ask questions. The doctor said he would keep them informed and continued on his rounds.

While Mama and Papa walked down the hall, Arturo stayed behind. He stopped at the nurses' station and asked, "Has my brother, I mean Francisco Morales, had any visitors other than us?"

The woman behind the desk turned some pages in a record book. "No," she said. "I don't see any. Of course they may not have checked in."

Arturo thanked her and walked quickly to catch up with his parents. It was very strange, he thought. Why hadn't Francisco's buddies come to see him?

Mama and Papa had stopped by a little chapel in the hospital. "Let's say a prayer for Francisco." Mama took Papa's hand and walked into the dark, quiet room. The small, flickering candles in the front cast a warm, golden glow around the darkened room. Arturo knelt down. He felt so much better now that Francisco recognized them and spoke to them—even if it was so little. He prayed silently: Please, dear Jesus, help make my brother well. And please help us find out who shot him. Arturo didn't dare think of what he might do if he found out who had shot Francisco. He tried to keep angry thoughts out of his mind while he was praying, but he couldn't help but feel angry with *El Lobo* for not coming to see his brother. Suddenly, another thought entered Arturo's mind. As long as he was here, praying, he would ask for help with something else. But no, he shouldn't be thinking of anything other than Francisco's getting well.

Arturo felt safe and secure in the hospital chapel. Francisco wouldn't care if he made an additional request. So, swallowing hard, Arturo continued his prayer, moving his lips silently: Please, Jesus, could you also help Mr. Moreno get Mrs. Edmonds to sell the land to us for a lot less if we give her cash? Arturo felt funny about asking, but he continued his prayer. We've come so far with our park, and we want to finish it—for the little kids, he added, thinking of Juanita.

CHAPTER 20

IT WAS BARELY DAYLIGHT when Arturo woke up the next morning. All night he had dreamed about Francisco and finding who shot him. Maybe if he talked to Francisco in the morning, he would have more strength. Maybe if Mama and Papa weren't there, Francisco would tell him what had happened. He had to try. Quickly dressing for school, Arturo slipped out quietly to catch the bus.

At the hospital, the lady at the information desk told him that Francisco was out of intensive care and in a regular room. When Arturo walked anxiously into his brother's room, there was Francisco sitting up, eating breakfast.

"Little brother!" Francisco said weakly, then put his cup down on the tray.

"Man, you look well enough to come home, Francisco!" Arturo's tennis shoes squeaked across the slick floor. He was thrilled to see Francisco alert, even though he was still pale. Arturo climbed onto the stool next to the bed and gave Francisco a gentle hug as if he might break if he weren't careful. Happiness flowed into Arturo and filled him. He started rattling on about the park project: the lunch, the money, how Mr. Khourian had asked if he was going to be a landscape architect. "Do you think I could, Francisco?"

Francisco smiled weakly and looked at Arturo seriously.

"I was wrong, *hermano.*" His voice was sad.

"About the park, you mean, Francisco?"

"About the park and . . . lots of other things. I didn't

think we could do . . . anything important. . . . I thought the *Vatos* . . ."

Arturo was serious now. "I didn't believe it either, Francisco. But Mr. Moreno and Miss Fenwick said—"

"I was wrong about other things, too," Francisco's eyes were barely open. He lay back on his pillow as if he were very tired even this early in the morning. He turned his head away.

"Francisco," Arturo lowered his voice and squeezed his brother's hand. "If we buy our land, maybe you can come see our park."

"That wouldn't be a good idea." Francisco didn't even open his eyes. "They are . . . they . . ."

Arturo looked at his brother sagging back against the pillow. His new moustache had been shaved off so that the cut on his lip where he had hit the sidewalk could be sewed up. The only whiskers he had were the ends of stitches. With the elation over Francisco's being able to talk, Arturo had momentarily forgotten what he had come to ask. Now he remembered. "Who did it, Francisco? Who shot you?"

Francisco didn't answer. He seemed drowsy after his exertion. Arturo squeezed his hand harder. "Tell me, Francisco! Don't you know? I want to help the *Vatos* find him."

Francisco turned his head toward Arturo surprisingly quickly. "No, Arturo, don't do . . . I . . . I was wrong." Francisco's eyes closed slowly and his voice trailed off. "About . . . everything."

"I'll be back soon, Francisco." Arturo squeezed his hand again and slowly walked out. Even though Francisco couldn't talk much yet, he was better. There weren't any tubes or wires attached to him. Arturo was relieved to see him a little stronger. Arturo and the other *Vatos* were going to find whoever did this to his brother and get even. Arturo felt the anger return. He needed to find Lobo right away. Then suddenly Francisco's words came back to him. "I was wrong about everything." What did he mean?

When Arturo got off the bus, Maria walked toward him. Pretending he didn't see her, Arturo hurried inside the school before she caught up.

"Hey Arturo! I've got something to tell you."

He rushed inside the classroom and sat down. Yeah, she probably wanted to follow him around, telling him that she and Angel had had a fight, but he was not interested.

Arturo looked up to see Mr. Moreno sitting on Miss Fenwick's desk. He wasn't due to come to class until tomorrow, but there he was. Miss Fenwick had scooted her chair to the side so she could see around him. He looked very serious, with his ankles crossed and his arms crossed on his chest.

Arturo took a deep, heavy breath. Mr. Moreno definitely didn't look like he had good news. Arturo didn't want to hear bad news. Juanita looked really discouraged.

"Well, class, I did my best." Mr. Moreno said, his voice solemn. "I talked to the lot's owner, Mrs. Ethel Edmonds, on the phone practically all of last evening. I tried every possible way to convince her to reduce the price. I appealed to her philanthropic feelings. I told her that it would help many children like you all to have a safe, attractive place to play and enjoy. I told her that if we paid the price she asked, we would have no money to build our park, so why would we buy the land?" Mr. Moreno frowned as if he were really troubled. He jiggled one foot, then started walking in a circle, punching one palm with his other fist.

Fear prickled outward from Arturo's stomach and

through his whole body as he thought of all their work. They were so close. He looked around the room. Every student's attention was absolutely glued to Mr. Moreno, who was sitting down on the desk again. The room was so silent that when Mr. Moreno punched his fist into his hand again, it sounded like an explosion.

"I offered her forty thousand dollars in cash, but she said we would have to stick to our agreed price of fifty-nine thousand dollars. We talked and talked some more, and . . ."

Clorissa's brows creased with fear.

"And . . ." Mr. Moreno lifted his arm high and leaped into the air and his shirt came out of his pants in front. "She accepted!"

The class sat quietly for a moment, looking at each other with puzzled expressions. Then, after realizing they'd been had, they erupted from their seats. Only Clorissa was not jumping. She was wiping her eyes, crying and laughing all at once. "Mr. Moreno, you're mean. Why did you make us think we didn't get it?"

Mr. Moreno laughed some more, then swung his arms around. He was crazy with joy. Arturo looked at him and realized that Mr. Moreno had been a kid like them once— maybe he still was. Miss Fenwick was laughing and clapping, too.

"I'm sorry, kids. I just couldn't resist teasing you." He threw punches into the air. "Isn't it grrrrrrreat?"

Suddenly Arturo looked at Trevor, and they understood each other without a word. Trevor passed the look on to LeDru and Angel. In about ten seconds, every boy and some of the girls rushed around Mr. Moreno and pounded him with mock-angry punches.

"Help! Help!" he yelled. Instead of getting help, others ran up and started punching, too. Juanita crowded between Arturo and Trevor and punched him on the thigh. Clorissa gave him a solid one on the upper arm. Arturo drew away from the dogfight and jumped around like a boxer. He looked over to see Miss Fenwick laughing. Suddenly Arturo realized that because she was always so quiet and sweet, people didn't always notice how hard she worked to help them. Everyone was punching Mr. Moreno as if he had done all the work.

"Go punch him, Miss Fenwick!" Arturo gave her a little push toward Mr. Moreno. "I'll bet he fooled you, too."

As she walked up to the jumping, punching group, LeDru yelled, "We'll hold him. You sock him, Miss Fenwick."

"Oh, no, help! help!" Mr. Moreno pleaded. Then, when she gave him a ladylike punch in the stomach that wouldn't have hurt a mosquito, he doubled up and gasped as if he'd been killed.

Miss Fenwick covered her mouth and laughed and laughed.

"Ha! You call that a punch?" Angel rushed forward again, but Miss Fenwick grabbed him around the waist.

"We've had enough fun beating up on Mr. Moreno, students."

"Yeah, let's beat up on Angel now," LeDru said, and everyone laughed but just sat down, panting from exertion.

Mr. Moreno pushed his hair out of his eyes, took a deep breath, and got serious. He said he also had told Mrs. Edmonds that no one else would want the land because of its location. She had finally agreed to the lower price for cash as a donation to the children of Southwood Elementary School.

"Shouldn't we have a party to celebrate?" asked Trevor. "My parents went to a groundbreaking ceremony once, I remember."

"Right!" Angel seemed eager for a party.

"Okay," said Miss Fenwick. "Let's plan a groundbreaking party next week when Mr. Moreno comes again."

LeDru started out their planning session the next week with a bang. "Let's invite everybody in the neighborhood!" he said.

"Yes, yes," Juanita said eagerly. "Mr. and Mrs. Lopez and their children. Mrs. Lopez helped get names for our petition, even though it didn't work."

Everyone was so fired up that it didn't take long to plan the party. "Let's make some tee shirts to sell," Maria suggested. Arturo agreed to make a design for the shirts. Juanita and Clorissa volunteered to write a flyer to invite everyone in the neighborhood.

"Let's invite Father Miller from St. Augustine's Church to dedicate our land," Arturo suggested.

"And shouldn't somebody give a talk, Miss Fenwick?" Trevor waved his hand wildly.

"Who would you suggest?" she asked. After they voted, Clorissa was chosen to speak, and Trevor was selected to read something.

"We have to be quick and start creating the park because it's almost February and school will be out in about four months," Clorissa reminded everyone.

"But now that we have the money for the land, we have everything we need for our park!" Juanita said.

"Except the zoning. Mr. Chesterton said that we still need permission from the city," said Angel.

"Oh, Angel! We won't have any problem. You are always so negative." Juanita looked annoyed.

That day was the most wonderful day Arturo could remember. When Maria caught up to him on his way home, he didn't even try to get away. "Arturo, Arturo," she yelled. She wasn't all flirty smiles like she usually was. She looked serious, even frightened. When she got up close, she whispered, low and out of breath, "I know where Lobo is. Angel told me."

"He knew all along. That little punk!"

"Yeah, he doesn't want me to tell you, but I liked Francisco. He was great. One time when I was little he played hopscotch with me. If I can help Francisco, I will." She took a gulp of air. "Who cares what Angel thinks. I'm mad at him."

Arturo frowned. He didn't like the way she spoke about Francisco as if he were dead.

CHAPTER 21

THE GRAY MORNING was still silent when Arturo stepped out of his apartment building the next morning. An occasional car streaked by on the freeway overhead, but serious morning traffic had not yet begun, and the streets were empty. Maria had said that Mirasol Lane was where Lobo hung out. He had to get there before Lobo left for the day.

The sky was lightening to white smog as Arturo trotted and ran through the empty streets. When he turned the corner and entered onto Mirasol, a little dead-end street, a *rincon* that didn't go anywhere, a wall of dank, moldy-smelling air hit Arturo's face. Swallowing hard, he wrinkled his nose to keep from gagging from the stench of the rotting garbage along the curb, the reek of urine, and the mustiness of a place that hadn't been cleaned by fresh air in years.

What was Lobo doing in a place like this? Arturo wondered. This wasn't where Francisco used to stay with him and his other *compas*. As he approached the address Maria had given him, he realized that he was heading toward an abandoned industrial building. A worn sign on its brick wall said "Superior Tennis Sho . . ." with a corroded painting of a laced-up tennis shoe. Higher up a number of windows were broken. Arturo felt uneasy. He was used to dumpy places, but this was abandoned, dangerous looking. He cautiously walked up to the big garage-type door. He felt like running away, but when he thought of his brother in that hospital bed, he stepped forward again. He knocked on the peeling green paint of the door. The door rattled on its hinges, but no one responded.

"Lobo, I know you are there," he said. "I want to talk to you. Please, I want to help the *Vatos*. Let me do it, Lobo. I want to help you get whoever shot Francisco." There was no sound from within. He felt funny talking to a door.

"Let me in, Lobo. *Por favor, compa.* I want to help you."

Arturo heard the sound of someone moving around quietly. Arturo walked to the side of the building, put his foot on a ledge in the wall, and pulled himself up by grabbing a wire fence near it. Looking through a broken window, Arturo saw Lobo standing by a wadded-up sleeping bag, his hair uncombed and on end. He held a gun in his hand, and it was pointed at Arturo.

"Hey, Lobo, it's me, Arturo. Remember how you invited me to join the *Vatos,* so now I—"

"Beat it, *niño,*" said Lobo. "We don't need any wanna-bes in the *Vatos.* Go on home."

"Let me help. Why are you here, Lobo? Why aren't—"

"Listen!" Lobo sounded menacing. "We have our own way of handling these things. We don't need help from babies. Get out of here right now, or you can never join the *Vatos.*"

Arturo slid down the brick wall, landing with one foot on a beer bottle. His heart was beating like a speeding motor.

Inside the building, Lobo was talking, his voice still low and menacing. "Beat it, *niño,* I mean it."

Puzzled and upset, Arturo shook his head and left.

"We have our own way of handling these things," Lobo had said. He must have thought that Arturo was too young to help, but that wasn't true. Lobo was probably lying in ambush waiting to get one of the Thirty-thirders. But he, Arturo, wanted to avenge the attack on his brother.

On Monday, after feeling tense for two days over his run-in with Lobo, Arturo began to breathe a little easier once he got to school. The classroom was like a different, better world. Soon he was caught up again in planning the ground-breaking ceremony, although images of both Francisco and Lobo kept flashing through his mind, off and on, which kept him in a troubled state.

Contacting all the people involved with the park project took more time than they had expected, so the class decided to hold the groundbreaking dedication for the park on the Saturday after next. That way people who worked during the week could come.

And on that Saturday, they did come. More than two hundred people stood around the dump among abandoned, beat-up car hulks and sofas overflowing with stuffing. Mama and Papa walked beside Francisco protectively as if he were their new *niño*. Francisco had made so much progress that the doctors let him come home. He was pale and thin but getting stronger. Arturo watched him anxiously while he himself strutted around, proudly dressed like the rest of his classmates in a tee shirt he had designed and the class had printed. There was a drawing of a tree and a swing on the front and the words, "We did it!" On the back, in Spanish, were the words, *"¡Sí! ¡Lo hicimos!"*

Arturo carried a big sign that he had made, saying, "Hurray for our park!" Another sign said, "Thank you, Mr. Chesterton." In among the kids from the school, teachers, families, Mr. and Mrs. Chesterton, and neighbors were TV cameramen and newspaper reporters.

Mrs. Lopez pushed a stroller with little Consuelo, wearing brand new tiny gold earrings, in it. Mrs. Lopez was wearing a new dress with pink roses on it, which looked as if it had a small watermelon under it—her baby was due in a couple of months. Mr. Lopez held an older boy's hand.

"How do you feel now that your class has raised enough money for the land?" a reporter asked Arturo.

"Proud!" Arturo said, "Real proud!"

Lots of smiling, happy grown-ups also seemed proud. Papa had put on his best white shirt for the occasion. He looked bewildered, as if he couldn't believe what was happening. Arturo felt important as he walked over to Miss Fenwick.

"Your kids have done a fine job," said a heavy-set man in a bright print shirt with palm trees on it. "It would be nice if—" He hadn't finished his sentence when a red-haired woman crowded in front of him and Arturo. "Yes, it would be nice to have a couple of those concrete block stoves in the park so families could have barbecues." She was speaking to Miss Fenwick as if she expected her to answer.

Juanita turned around when she heard the woman and joined Arturo. The woman ignored Arturo and Juanita but smiled at Miss Fenwick. "It would also be nice to have a table and some chairs or stools where older people could sit and play checkers. A horseshoe area would be nice, too."

Juanita and Arturo looked at each other angrily, then Arturo said, "I think that . . ." but no one looked at him or listened. The adults talked faster and faster above his head. He heard Juanita's voice squeaking, "That isn't what . . ." but no one paid any attention.

The talk was interrupted by music from one of Trevor's

tapes, and Clorissa got up and stood on a ragged hunk of concrete that she was using for a speaker's podium.

"I want everyone to know how proud and happy I am to belong to a group like this that has accomplished so much. The result shows what great and noble things people can do when they work together. I am going to remember this all my life, and I know that the little children of this neighborhood will love playing in this park."

Then Trevor came forward and read a selection from the Bible. He stood straight and confident in his blue polo shirt while the breeze blew his yellow hair. The words sounded perfect to Arturo. "The wilderness and the solitary place shall be glad for them; and the desert shall rejoice, and blossom as the rose. It shall blossom abundantly and rejoice even with joy and singing." Arturo smiled when he thought about how the dump certainly wasn't a wilderness or a desert but the words made him want to burst into song anyway.

Mr. Moreno made a few comments, and Miss Fenwick said that it had been her pleasure to act as a helper to the class. She added, "This project really belongs to the students."

Next, Father Miller from St. Augustine's Church came up front. Everyone stopped giggling and chattering, and Arturo could hear only the swish, rrrroom, rumbling undertones of the freeway interchange overhead. Father Miller stood silently for a moment against the muted background accompaniment, then began a prayer for the success of the project. Many in the audience didn't understand English very well, so he spoke slowly and clearly while Juanita stood beside him and translated his words into Spanish.

"This doesn't look like a park," Father Miller said, "but

it is a park. This is a park in spirit, consecrated by the hard work and love of this class of children, their teachers, and many generous spirits who have donated their help to make this day possible." Arturo held his breath in rapt attention. No one made a sound.

Then Father Miller held up a plastic gallon jug. "I have brought this water, which has been blessed, to sprinkle over the land to consecrate and dedicate it. Each of you, please, help us to begin cleansing and purifying this land by gathering some of the unwanted items, discarded here in our park, into one pile."

A storm of applause and cheering followed Father Miller's words. Arturo scrambled to grab a rusted exhaust manifold. Mrs. Lopez steered the baby stroller with one hand while dragging a huge piece of gray cardboard to the rapidly growing pile. A caterpillar-like sofa carcass running on twelve legs was actually being carried by three kids on either side. Trevor, LeDru, and Clorissa added the framework of a filing cabinet, and Arturo threw on a ragged tire.

Men piled the junk into trucks lent by the businesses that employed some of them as well as into a couple of beat-up old pickups from the neighborhood.

Mr. Chesterton rolled up the long sleeves of his shirt, and the breeze blew his white hair as he carried a rusty brake drum in one hand and an exhaust pipe in the other. Mrs. Chesterton dragged a chunk of stained brown carpet. Francisco leaned over to pick up a car bumper but stood up uncomfortably with an expression of pain and a hand on his chest. Arturo quickly rushed over to him, and Papa followed. The three of them dragged the big hunk of metal to the pile, but Francisco looked pale and stood without moving. Mama put her arm around him. "You'd better go rest now, son."

As Arturo and Francisco turned to cross the street to their apartment, Francisco stopped suddenly. Arturo looked up to see Lobo and a couple of the *Vatos* driving by in Lobo's car, the Midnight Cruiser. Lobo wasn't driving.

"Move into the crowd," Francisco said, walking back into the throng of people. Lobo, in a black-and-white plaid shirt and black bandanna, was riding shotgun. With his elbow on the window, Lobo looked intensely through his black glasses, as if he were looking for someone.

"Walk," Francisco said urgently, and with surprising strength, Francisco pulled Arturo back with him into the crowd.

"But they are your buddies," Arturo said, puzzled.

"Quiet! Keep walking!" Francisco frowned into Arturo's upturned face and tightened his grip.

CHAPTER 22

"**BUT, FRANCISCO**, that was Lobo and your buddies." Arturo was puzzled and disturbed.

"They are no friends of mine anymore." Francisco seemed nervous and shaken.

"But they have to be!" Arturo's heart beat quicker. "When you joined them, Francisco, you promised to protect and help each other forever and . . . and . . ." He tried to sort out his thoughts. What had his brother done? Why had he been kicked out? "You promised to be *compas* for life—for life, Francisco!" Arturo looked pleadingly at his brother.

Francisco walked silently and quickly across the street toward their apartment as soon as the Cruiser disappeared around the corner.

"Aren't they trying to find the guy who shot you, Francisco? They promised." Arturo trotted to keep up. "I went to Lobo and asked if I could help, and . . ." In his excitement, Arturo told Francisco about his trip to Mirasol Lane.

Francisco stopped at the bottom of the stairs and caught his breath, putting his hand on his chest. "No, little brother! Listen to me! Stay away from Lobo. Stay away, do you hear?"

Mama and Papa were waiting in the apartment. Much to Arturo's surprise, Francisco told them about the *Vatos* and the Cruiser and their getting away from them.

"If those guys are after you in this barrio, Francisco, you should leave." Papa walked back and forth in front of the couch where Francisco was sitting. Papa didn't seem to know that the guys were Francisco's gang brothers. Then again, maybe he didn't want to know.

"Leave, Papa? I have no place to go."

"Listen to your father, Francisco," Mama said. "Papa and I want you to go live with Aunt Yolanda and Uncle Juan in El Monte. They said you could stay with them, and Aunt Yolanda says they have a continuation school. You can go back and finish high school." Mama smiled and patted Francisco on the hand.

Arturo sat quietly, listening, thinking of what Francisco had told him. Questions he was afraid to ask kept running through his mind.

"Or you can get a real job!" Papa said.

Mama turned and frowned at Papa.

Francisco seemed broken. His body had been injured, but even worse, his spirit seemed wounded, too. He used to strut around so cool. He used to say that Mama and Papa didn't know anything, that they were too old fashioned and Mexican. Now he was sitting quietly and listening to them as if he didn't think they were dumb at all.

"I'll think about it, Mama."

"Uh-huh, don't think so long that you are shot again before you decide. Shot dead next time! Do you hear?" Papa's eyes were fierce as he shook his finger angrily at Francisco. Arturo had never seen him that mad before. "You go to El Monte with your Aunt Yolanda and Uncle Juan."

". . . finish high school." Mama said, finishing the sentence.

"Huh!" Papa huffed. "I didn't go to school. Let him get a real job!"

"I will think about it," Francisco said. He looked up quickly as if he had remembered something important.

That night Arturo went to bed without talking to Francisco. He was so upset by what he had heard that he felt sick. How could the *Vatos* not be Francisco's friends anymore? Didn't they swear to always be there for each other? Wasn't that the whole reason?

Arturo never thought he would feel eager to get to school every day. Their park project was unfolding so smoothly. Something real was being built—not torn down, not covered with garbage. No one was getting shot, killed, or injured. No, he was helping to create something new that people needed and enjoyed. This project felt so good, especially compared to all the worries he had about Francisco.

"Do you have a drawing of your park layout to show the student architect?" Miss Fenwick asked Arturo. "She's coming to talk with you in a couple weeks. She needs your ideas in order to prepare a drawing for the building department."

"Here it is." Arturo held up his drawing.

"Good, Arturo. Now remember what we talked about," Miss Fenwick said to the class. "It is your park. You all are the architect's clients. Work with her to help the layout represent your ideas. Plan what you want to tell Ms. Otaro-Schultz."

"You said it is our project, Miss Fenwick. Is it really still ours?" Juanita was unusually serious.

"Darn right it is," said LeDru. "We didn't do all this work for nothing."

"But I heard one of my neighbors saying to another

lady," Juanita continued, "that she was going to ask the school principal if they would put in barbecue grills and tables for families."

Trevor's hand waved wildly. "Mr. Chesterton said people talked to him about stuff they wanted in the park, too."

"One lady said she was starting a neighborhood group to meet Tuesday night to talk about what they wanted in the park." Maria sounded angry.

Everybody looked at Maria with surprise. She hardly ever took part.

"I'm glad they're interested in the park," Clorissa said reasonably. "But I don't want them to take control of our project."

"Adults always think they know best," Juanita said. She tossed a braid over her shoulder angrily.

"And they always want to run things," LeDru added.

Arturo was about to say something when he remembered that Miss Fenwick was an adult. But she had always encouraged them to speak up and to have ideas. Maybe her feelings would be hurt if they talked like this around her.

"Have these people tried to take the park project from you?" Miss Fenwick spoke in a serious voice.

"No, but they might!" Angel sounded fierce. For Angel to care about the park seemed to surprise everyone.

"You students have been in charge all along. I'm sure you can keep control," Miss Fenwick said. "Mrs. Ochoa, the lady you mentioned, invited me to the Tuesday-night meeting, and I went. A lot of neighborhood people came. I'm glad that they are interested."

The kids sat quietly. "But why didn't she invite us?" Arturo asked. "It's our project!" He had expected Miss Fenwick to take their side.

"Yeah, it's our project!" "We started it!" "Why weren't we all invited?" A clamor of voices was followed by Clorissa's clear statement. "I think it was rude and inconsiderate not to invite us. What do you think, Miss Fenwick?"

Miss Fenwick always looked on the good side of things, but now she frowned. "Girls and boys, the people are excited about the park actually being built, and that is good. But it's true that they now have their own ideas for it." Miss Fenwick paused, as though she were troubled. "One lady said it was wonderful how much you children had done, but that now the park needed adult managers. She wanted her neighborhood group to be those managers."

"That's a crummy thing to say. Look at what 'us kids' have done already," said Trevor.

Miss Fenwick frowned again. "I didn't say anything at their meeting, boys and girls. But now I am saying that I agree it is your park project and you should not let them take it from you. It is time to assert yourselves."

"But what can we do?" asked Arturo. "We are just kids, and they are grown-ups."

"I have been thinking, class. This is the time for another real-life lesson—in management. How can people keep control of their own lives and surroundings? Do we have any way for people to do that in our country?"

"We vote on things," Arturo said. "And we vote against things we don't want." Miss Fenwick had taught him that.

"But not everybody can vote on every little thing in the state or even in the city," Juanita said.

"That's why we elect representatives," Clorissa stated, "to the House of Representatives and the Senate and things."

"Right! Right! But how does that work with us and our

park? How do we make people who suggest things let us vote on whether we want to do those things or not?" Clorissa asked.

"Let me give you a suggestion, class. Then we'll talk about it and vote on whether or not to do it." Miss Fenwick said. "Sometimes businesses and organizations elect a board of directors to represent the whole company. The people on the board are elected by the people who own the company. The people who own the company are called shareholders because they own parts, or shares, of the organization. Shareholders can vote for people on the board. They can also suggest ideas to the board. Then the board votes on them." Miss Fenwick waited for the students' responses, which came immediately.

"Good! Good! Let's elect a board of directors." Juanita waved her hand wildly.

"Then the neighborhood people will have to give their ideas to us to vote on because we started the whole thing and have control of the funds." Trevor laughed and wiggled delightedly.

"That's the idea, Trevor," Miss Fenwick concluded. "Now let's vote on whether or not you want to elect a board of directors."

"Let's do it." Clorissa's approval was followed by a chorus of voices chanting, "Let's do it! Let's do it!"

The idea to form an organization and elect a board of directors passed without any problem. Then all of the kids—the shareholders—elected individual students to make up the board of directors.

Clorissa was elected chairperson of the board; Trevor, vice chairperson; Juanita, secretary; and LeDru, treasurer.

The board's first action was to ask for suggestions for committees that needed to be formed, and then for people to be committee heads. Arturo was selected to be the head of the design committee.

The second action was to decide that all park suggestions first had to be approved by the board of directors in order to be included in the park. When the motion passed, Juanita stomped on the floor with joy.

"Now they can't steal our project," Arturo said and waved his hand high in triumph.

"We need a name for our company," LeDru said.

"It isn't a company, is it, Miss Fenwick?" Trevor asked. "We aren't running a business."

"That's true, Trevor, because you are not selling anything or trying to make any money."

"We are a philanthropical organization," Clorissa stated with pride.

The shareholders discussed names and decided to call their organization "The Southwood Community Association."

"Terrific, kids." Miss Fenwick looked as happy as they did. "Now we can start actually creating the park!"

"I can hardly wait!" said Arturo.

"You won't have to wait long, Arturo. One week from this morning Ms. Otaro-Schultz is coming to confer with us."

"Confer! I like that word. It sounds important." Juanita giggled.

On the way home that afternoon, Arturo thought about the fact that the class had kept control of their project. All suggestions had to go through them. Miss Fenwick was so smart. And he was the head of the design committee!

Juanita walked along with him and asked about Francisco. Arturo said that he was better, but a shiver went through him as he thought of the question he hadn't yet dared to ask Francisco.

CHAPTER 23

THE DAY Ms. Otaro-Schultz was coming to meet with him, Arturo put on his new white shirt and his blue sweater-vest. Glimpsing himself in the mirror, he decided he looked more businesslike than in his Dodgers tee shirt. "I'll do all right. I'll do all right," he told himself. Hadn't he done all right at the luncheon?

Francisco was still asleep. He was getting well, though slowly. Rolling over, he woke up and looked at Arturo. "What's happening, little brother?"

"I'm head of the design committee for the park. I have to talk to the architecture student who's going to work with us." Arturo's chest expanded proudly.

Francisco pushed the hair back from his forehead. "Do a good job." He didn't look happy.

Boy, had Francisco changed, Arturo thought. With some water on a comb, he forced the hair on the back of his head to lie down. "I'll try," he said to Francisco. One tuft of hair popped up.

He was so early leaving for school that Maria wasn't there to tag along. Arturo went down the steps quietly, saying over and over in his head, "I'll do all right."

Ms. Caroline Otaro-Schultz was a slender young woman with dark hair and eyes and golden brown skin. She wore a bright blue suit and carried a notepad and purse. Arturo thought she looked nervous. Her nervousness made him feel braver.

After Miss Fenwick greeted her and nodded to Arturo,

165

he walked over and held out his hand. "I am Arturo Morales, head of the design committee." He pronounced each word carefully. "I would like to welcome you on behalf of the Southwood Community Association." Arturo's voice squeaked when he said "behalf," but he finished the whole introduction without a mistake. Taking a deep breath, he relaxed into a smile and shook her hand while she smiled shyly in return. She had Mexican coloring, but she didn't quite look Mexican. Feeling really important, Arturo showed her to a chair in the front of the classroom with the board of directors and then sat down beside her.

Ms. Otaro-Schultz started asking questions. "What kind of activities do you want kids to be able to do in your park?"

Arturo knew just what to say. "We all decided that our park is too small to have everything. We want it to be just for young kids, kids in preschool and elementary school—kids the age we were while we were at Southwood School." His voice didn't squeak once. Juanita smiled at him.

"Some people want volleyball nets and basketball hoops, too," Juanita said.

"But if big kids come in, the little kids will get crowded out or scared off." Clorissa spoke firmly.

"So we want swings, slides, and a sand box to dig in and to make roads and stuff. A teeter-totter, too, and a jungle gym to climb on would be nice. And lots of bushes, trees, and flowers." Arturo felt sure of himself now.

Ms. Otaro-Schultz looked at Arturo's design. "And you want two rest rooms, right?"

"I guess so," Arturo said, sounding uncertain.

Angel held up his hand.

Arturo was afraid of what Angel would say but called on him anyway.

166

"Don't put in any rest rooms. Rest rooms are good places for drug dealers to hang out. There shouldn't be any tall solid things that you can't see through, either. Dealers like to hide behind stuff."

What a surprise, Arturo thought, that Angel had had a real idea, not just a wise-guy crack. Arturo laughed. "Kids run home to the bathroom now, so I guess they can keep on doing it."

Ms. Otaro-Schultz looked startled. "I wouldn't have thought of that. But you know the neighborhood better than I do."

Arturo looked at Angel. Now that the park project was successful, everyone wanted to be on the team. But he felt sure that Angel knew about the drug business. A picture of Lobo in the Cruiser suddenly came into his mind, and he felt angry again.

When Ms. Otaro-Schultz left, she said that she would have "working drawings" in about a month. "I'd like to do them sooner, but I am swamped getting my senior project ready, too."

After the interview and during their wait for the drawings, there was still a lot the board members had to do, including examining the playground-equipment catalogs that Mr. Chesterton had brought.

"Last time he was here, Mr. Chesterton said he was still working on the zoning permission," Clorissa said.

"So we don't even have permission to build the park yet?" LeDru asked. "What will we do if we don't get it?"

"Let's just do what we can now." Clorissa wasn't going to be discouraged.

They decided to ask three qualified surveyors, excavating contractors, and concrete contractors to give them prices. Mr.

Chesterton had said builders usually asked for "bids" from at least three companies and usually took the lowest bid.

During the fun, Arturo felt a pang of guilt as he remembered Francisco. He had to find his brother's attacker. People can't get away with stuff like that, he thought. But visions of the finished park with kids playing in it continued to form in his mind. They had to finish the park in time for graduation.

Juanita, as secretary of the board, was responsible for writing letters to the contractors and thank-yous to the donors. After a couple of weeks of it she said, "Shouldn't we have stationery like real organizations do?"

"Have Arturo make a design," said Trevor.

"Maybe other people would like to try designing, too," Miss Fenwick suggested. "There are other good artists in the class."

"Okay, since I'm head of design, I'll have a contest." Arturo raised his eyebrows self-importantly. "I'll pick the winner. But don't put your name on your design."

By the end of the art period that day, seven drawings had been submitted.

The design Arturo picked had a big fluffy cloud by a tree with a smiling sun peeking out around it. Arching over the top like a rainbow were the words, "Southwood Community Association."

He was surprised to find that the winning design was Maria's.

Miss Fenwick and Maria went to the office and made copies of her design for stationery. Arturo thought it looked great! He felt as pleased as if he had done it himself.

The day the surveyor they had chosen came, the whole class

walked to the lot. Kids took turns looking through the sextant while the surveyor explained that he was locating the property lines and seeing how level the land was.

Then one warm April morning before school, as Arturo munched on a tortilla, he heard the deep rumble of heavy equipment. He shot out the door, down the steps, and onto the sidewalk, nearly falling over a doll on the stairway.

Trucks and earth-moving equipment were coming down the street. Maria came running outside, too. "Hey! I could see them from the window. Look!"

They stood on the curb and watched workmen loading big chunks of concrete onto the hydraulic tailgate of a truck. A bulldozer smoothed another part of the dump.

Neighbors poured out of the apartment building to watch. Mrs. Lopez had two of her little ones hanging onto her.

After the lot was cleaned, the place looked strange and wonderful. They smoothed the ground until it reminded Arturo of a big, blank piece of paper, waiting for a design. A shiver of excitement ran through him.

Maria and Arturo looked at each other with amazement. What they were seeing didn't seem real. Arturo ran back to his apartment. He had to tell Francisco. As Arturo burst into the living room, Francisco was walking toward him, slowly, carefully, like an old man. Arturo ran to him. "Come look, Francisco, it's really happening. You said we could never do it, remember? But we're really doing it." Arturo jumped into the air and made a punching motion.

"I was wrong, Arturo, wrong about a lot of things," Francisco said. "I've been thinking, uh, the police came yesterday and talked to me. I told them I didn't know anything, but . . . but . . ."

But Arturo had already started running off to school and barely heard Francisco say, "After school. Let's talk about it, okay?"

On Friday afternoon Mr. Chesterton asked them what equipment they wanted to order for their park. "I've brought lots of good news, too," he said, looking cramped sitting in such a small chair. "People continue to call my office, wanting to donate money. Here, I brought twelve hundred dollars more in checks."

"That's great," said LeDru, who was the treasurer. He took the checks. "Thank you. Wow! We are floating in money!"

"People have also offered to donate materials and labor," Mr. Chesterton continued. "The California Horticulturist Association wants to give you the trees and plants. They will do the planting for what it costs to pay their workers."

"Sure, you got to pay workers," LeDru said.

"Now, about the zoning. This news isn't as good. Councilman Linden said it takes a long time to get things through. I told him that this was an emergency situation because you kids are graduating soon."

Arturo spoke up. "What if we don't get the zoning?"

"I don't think there will be any problem getting the zoning, but getting it in time might be hard. We probably aren't very high on the city council's list of things to do." Mr. Chesterton shrugged his shoulders. "We just have to hope for the best."

LeDru frowned. "It would be awful if we didn't get to see the park finished."

Arturo didn't want Mr. Chesterton to think they were ungrateful after all he had done, so he said, "You've been wonderful, Mr. Chesterton. We couldn't have gotten here without you."

A big wave of applause erupted. "Thank you, thank you, Mr. Chesterton, and thank Mrs. Chesterton, too."

Mr. Chesterton turned pink, as if he were embarrassed, then asked, "Have you chosen your playground equipment?"

LeDru opened the catalog of playground equipment to a colorful picture of an apparatus with a spiral of steps up to a slide. It also had a covered platform with swings below it. It had everything they were looking for.

"This is what we picked out, Mr. Chesterton." LeDru handed the catalog to him.

Mr. Chesterton seemed very shocked when he looked up. "This piece is really expensive. It costs twenty thousand dollars." Mr. Chesterton's jaw dropped and his mouth hung open with surprise.

"Wow!" Angel gasped. "You could buy a bunch of low riders with that."

No one on the board blinked. "We want it to be real nice for the little kids." Juanita was always worried about the "little kids." "It's a present that will last a long time."

Mr. Chesterton looked down and crossed his legs. "Well, I guess it's your money. And your project. If you want that one, that's the one we will order."

He seemed unusually quiet, Arturo thought.

"Since we are talking about equipment, I have a basketball backboard and basket in my yard that I would like to donate to the park." Mr. Chesterton smiled eagerly.

Clorissa's eyes grew large and concerned. She glanced over at Miss Fenwick, who didn't blink or smile.

Arturo looked at Clorissa. Everyone looked at Clorissa. All the shareholders looked distressed.

Clorissa studied the pencil in her hand carefully for a moment or two. She took a deep breath and then said, "Mr. Chesterton, you have done so much for us, and we appreciate how generous you are, but," she paused and swallowed, "we want our park to be just for little kids. Big kids would take it over. Thank you very much anyway for offering the hoop and backstop." She smiled sweetly.

Mr. Chesterton seemed startled. "Well, I just thought I'd offer it."

Arturo took a deep breath and relaxed. When Mr. Chesterton got up to leave, the class thanked him once again. As he stepped out the door, he waved. He wore his usual bright, cheery smile.

When his footsteps had faded down the hall, Miss Fenwick said, "Class and Madam Chairperson of the Board, congratulations. You did that nicely. You were strong but diplomatic."

"It was hard," Clorissa said. "Mr. Chesterton has done so much for us."

"Do you think we hurt his feelings, Miss Fenwick?" Juanita sounded troubled. "I don't want him to think we're ungrateful."

"He is probably as proud of you as I am to see you taking charge of your own lives and deciding things for yourselves."

Miss Fenwick always had a good way of saying things, Arturo thought. "Taking charge of your own lives." He liked the sound of it.

On his way home, Arturo walked with a springy bounce in his step. He felt as if he had done something important. He walked home a different route, and as he passed Trevor's house, he was startled by the sight of the words LOS VATOS

LOCOS spray painted in bloodred, *cholo* gang-style writing stretching from end to end of the wall he and Trevor had painted. Arturo stopped suddenly, as if he had been punched in the stomach. Those dirty, filthy wreckers! Were these his brother's sworn *compañeros*? They were wreckers— spoilers—just like the guys who come around with big concrete balls to break down buildings. Anger boiled up from his stomach and energized his arms. He wanted to punch out Francisco's whole *clika*. What was it, Arturo wondered, that Francisco had wanted to tell him?

CHAPTER 24

AT HOME Arturo found Francisco watching television. He looked a little stronger, but his expression was troubled.

"Hey, Arturo." Francisco grabbed his brother's arm, so Arturo pulled a chair up to the couch and sat down facing Francisco.

"Little brother." Francisco looked at a picture on the wall as though he didn't want to look at Arturo. "I don't want you to join a gang. Gangs—*clikas*—aren't cool. I thought they were, but look at me!" He turned to look at Arturo.

Arturo's heart beat faster, and his brow furrowed as he focused intently on his brother. "But, they help protect you and take care of you, and you are like brothers."

"That's what you think when you join. There is so much you don't know when you are a stupid wanna-be." Francisco's hand gripped Arturo's shoulder. His eyes were hard.

"They swear to be buddies for life, don't they?"

Francisco frowned angrily and took a deep breath, putting his hand up to his chest. He squeezed Arturo's arm hard and shook it.

"Buddies for life! Ha! Buddies for life, unless you try to leave."

"But, you wouldn't leave your *compas*."

"Listen to me, *estúpido*, this could save your life." In

a rush of angry words, Francisco told him that his *compañeros* had been great at first, but that he had gradually been dragged into doing things he wasn't proud of. "Pretty soon you are taking part in . . ." Francisco stopped and hung his head dejectedly.

Arturo shivered a little. He had wondered about these things, but he didn't like to have his brother's words make them real. "What about the guy who shot you?" Arturo asked angrily.

Francisco seemed weak and tired, but he looked up suddenly, his eyes blazing with anger. "I've been trying to tell you. My dear, lifelong-sworn *compas* shot me!"

Arturo's eyes opened wide, and his mouth began to quiver.

"Yes, my buddies shot me, not the Thirty-thirders."

Arturo did not answer.

"I wanted out of their dirty little outfit. I couldn't even stand to have Mama and Papa look at me. I tried to leave, and they went after me."

Arturo shivered again. "Who was it?" he demanded of his brother. "You can't let him get away with it!" Arturo demanded.

"I know."

"Who?" But Arturo already knew. Lobo hadn't been lying in ambush there on Mirasol. He was hiding from the police. "It was Lobo, wasn't it?"

Francisco didn't say anything but looked up at Arturo without protesting. It was as though the code still forbade him to tell on one of his former brothers.

Francisco slumped against the arm of the couch, his head turned away from Arturo as though he were completely used up.

"We have to do something, Francisco." Arturo squeezed his brother's arm.

On Monday as Arturo walked to school, he felt weak thinking of what Francisco had told him. He also felt somehow lighter and relieved. But he would do something, he had to. Lobo! What he had done was horrible.

As soon as he got to school, Arturo once again felt himself drawn into the project. Juanita came back from the office with a letter from Councilman Linden. She waved it high. "Hey look, guys, a certified letter from Councilman Linden came. I had to go sign for it." She ripped it open quickly. The zoning change had been granted.

Amid the cheers, LeDru held up his two fists like a prize fighter and shouted, "Yea for us!"

At last they could officially buy the property. LeDru, their treasurer, made out a check for forty thousand dollars plus escrow fees. Then Juanita signed it, Miss Fenwick cosigned it, and they passed it all around the class before taking it to the closing of the sale at the bank.

"Imagine! I can't believe that we did it!" Trevor said, looking at the check.

"I've never seen a check for even a hundred!" Arturo said.

The next day the concrete contractor came to tell them about laying the sidewalks. Arturo wanted to know exactly how everything was going to be done. This was his park. He felt like an owner. In a flash Francisco's troubled face came to him and with it came the understanding of what he had to do.

Tomorrow the whole class would watch the sidewalks being poured. Arturo looked around at his classmates all smiling and babbling excitedly.

"Are we going to have a big party when the park opens?" Angel asked eagerly.

Everyone was in favor of having a big party. Mr. Moreno voted with both hands.

"When will we get our jungle-gym equipment?" Trevor wanted to know about their super-expensive one-piece entertainment center.

"Who knows?" Arturo answered, but everyone else was ignoring the question. There was always another problem to worry about, thought Arturo, but the worry was worth it for something real and important.

Juanita said, "If the park isn't completed when we graduate, then a lot of us won't be around to celebrate. Trevor is moving in July, Maria and her family are going to visit relatives in Mexico, and Clorissa might be going to stay with her aunt for the summer." Everyone seemed to be thinking out loud.

Maria and Angel volunteered for the party committee.

"Hey, man, I don't mind that," Angel said.

"At last," LeDru sneered. "We've found something Angel likes to do."

Arturo felt certain that Angel knew about Lobo shooting Francisco. No wonder he didn't want him to know where Lobo was.

Arturo was glad he got home before Mama or Papa. He wanted to talk to Francisco, who was in the kitchen getting something to eat. "Francisco, I've been thinking about Lobo. We have to . . ." Arturo paused for strength, then looked up boldly and blurted out, "Francisco, we have to tell the police!" He felt better after he had said it and looked unblinkingly into Francisco's face. He was staring at Arturo— terrified.

Francisco looked down and, after a moment, said, "I'll think about it."

The park construction boomed along, and in a few weeks the workers had built concrete walks and a sandpit rim. The class came often to watch the whole plan become reality. Arturo couldn't believe how beautiful the curving walk looked.

One day in May a truck filled with potted trees and bushes pulled up to the curb. The sun was glinting off their bright green leaves. Arturo felt a burst of joy. The greenery looked so pretty, waiting to be planted in its new home. For the next few days, the kids went to the site and helped the nursery workers plant the trees, bushes, and flowers. Arturo picked up a trowel, got down on his knees, and planted a couple of flats of bright orange marigolds. They were the kind of flower he had seen that morning when Mr. Moreno first came. Those flowers had made Arturo realize that they needed a park. He had asked the board to request some marigolds. As the trowel blade dug into the soil, he wondered whether this was real or a dream.

Carefully, Arturo scooped out a ferny-leafed plant, put it into the hole in the dark earth, patted the dirt smoothly around it, and watered it thoroughly. Juanita and Maria were laying down rolls of lawn sod and watering them.

Arturo looked up at the red geraniums along the freeway fence and remembered the trash that had been there before. Was this really happening, he wondered?

While the kids worked, people in the neighborhood stopped and told them how wonderful they all were. Arturo laughed. A few months ago they had said how crazy they were.

That night Arturo was telling Francisco again that he must tell the police when Papa came in. "Tell the police what?" he asked, looking stern.

Arturo and Francisco looked at each other silently. "Tell him Francisco. Tell him, or I will." Arturo felt his fierce anger for Lobo rise up and give him strength.

The whole ugly story came tumbling out. Papa was furious, and Francisco was so upset by what he had had to tell that he burst into tears like a little kid. Mama came into the room and put her arms around him while Papa told her why Francisco had been shot.

"Tell the police, Francisco," Mama pleaded. "You have to." She held him while he sobbed.

Arturo turned aside. He couldn't stand to watch.

CHAPTER 25

ON THE MONDAY BEFORE GRADUATION, the class inspected the park. Benches were in place, the fence was up, and the trees, bushes, and flowers made it look like a dreamland. The sand had been poured into the play area. All that was needed to complete the design was the playground equipment, which still had not arrived.

"We can have our party," said Clorissa, "even without the equipment."

"But we want to see it!"

"Yeah!" a chorus of voices joined in.

"We worked hard on that park. We want to slide down that slide."

"And swing on those swings," somebody yelled.

"I'll call the guy we ordered it from at the manufacturer," said Trevor. "I'll tell him we're graduating this Friday!"

Trevor reported on Tuesday. The person at the manufacturer had said that they were behind in deliveries but would try to have the apparatus out by Thursday.

Thursday came and went without a delivery. The party had been planned for Sunday—two days after graduation, no matter what.

Somehow graduation seemed like a rehearsal for the "real" party, Arturo thought on Friday as he walked down the aisle to get his certificate. Trevor had called the company again on Thursday, and they had said that they would try their darndest to deliver the big apparatus before the party.

On Saturday, as Arturo came out of his apartment at about nine in the morning, he saw a large truck driving down La Luna very slowly. Arturo walked toward it on the sidewalk, and the driver stopped and looked out the window.

"Son, can you tell me where La Luna Children's Park is?"

The words sounded so wonderful that Arturo almost burst with joy. "Right across the street, down a little ways." he said, pointing. "Are you bringing equipment for it?"

"Sure am!"

Arturo had an urge to get Juanita. He began running toward her house as fast as he could and arrived out of breath.

Juanita ran most of the way back with him. They stood and watched while the men unlocked the fence and took the big pieces inside the park and bolted and riveted the enormous apparatus together. It was huge and brightly painted in the cheeriest red and blue. Arturo felt a rush of emotion as he thought of the dump that had been there before, and the fact that his class had changed it into a park. The change hadn't exactly been made with a magic wand. The process had been much harder and longer than a wave of a wand, but there was much more satisfaction this way. Juanita was crying and rubbing her eyes. "It's wonderful, so wonderful." Two of the youngest Lopez kids stood watching, transfixed with awe.

"Better give it a test drive," said one of the men. "Give your little sister and brother a ride," he said to Juanita and Arturo.

"Come on, *niño*." Arturo gestured to the little boy who

181

was about four years old. Leading him by the hand, Arturo lifted him onto the swing. Juanita put the little girl, who was about three, beside him onto the other swing, and they pushed them back and forth. The boy giggled and kicked. The girl hung on tightly, her eyes getting bigger and bigger.

The driver of the van chuckled. "Guess they work all right, kids, so we'd better go! We have to close the park now, so you'd better leave."

"Just a minute," Arturo said. He grabbed Juanita by the hand and led her to the stairway of the slide and let her go ahead of him. She scampered up the ladder and sat down, and Arturo sat down behind her. He put his arm around her so they could slide down together and jump out onto the sand. They laughed so hard they almost fell down. Then they took the two Lopez kids and left.

The big ribbon-cutting party the next day officially opened the park. If Aunt Yolanda and Uncle Juan would come over from El Monte with Francisco, Arturo thought, this would be absolutely the happiest day of his life. They had said they would try to come, but Francisco wasn't so sure he should chance a visit after he and Papa had gone to the police to tell them about Lobo.

The enormous, elaborate toy towered above everyone like a crown of triumph. Mr. and Mrs. Chesterton brought ice cream and hot dogs for everyone and hundreds of helium-filled balloons in a rainbow of colors. Bunches of balloons were tied to the apparatus, flocks of them floating high into the sky. Mr. Chesterton held a cluster that was like an enormous bunch of flowers. Arturo felt as light as a balloon. He thought that he might just float up and away.

Almost everyone in the neighborhood came to the party. Even Mayor Broderick came and said how delighted he was with this grassroots show of initiative. Councilman Linden, who had helped rush through the zoning, spoke of how proud he was of the people in his constituency. But, Arturo noticed, looking around anxiously, there wasn't any Francisco.

Mr. Moreno talked about how you can do great things if you believe in yourself. In her talk, Miss Fenwick said that accomplishing things helps build self-confidence, and self-confidence helps you accomplish things. She ended by saying, "Happy are those who dare to dream big dreams and are willing to work hard to make them come true."

Miss Fenwick was great! She had on a pretty white dress that almost fit her and some long, dangly hoop earrings. Arturo clapped until his hands hurt. He turned and smiled at Mama and Papa.

Clorissa talked about how everyone had grown so much in confidence and enthusiasm. "Our teachers made us realize we could do lots more than we thought we could." When she stepped down from the platform, slowly and proudly in her new blue dress, everyone clapped like thunder. Still no Francisco. Arturo looked down the street for his aunt and uncle's car.

After the speeches were over, all the kids lined up to initiate the equipment by climbing the ladder and going down the slide.

And there, in the park by a bench, Arturo stood and looked proudly at a large stone adorned with a plaque that Mr. and Mrs. Chesterton had ordered made. On it in bronze letters was a list of all the students who had helped make the park. Arturo read down to his name, "Arturo Morales."

"There, look, Mama! Papa!" He wanted to show it to Francisco. Where was he? He wanted to say, "Look, *hermano*, see what I helped do!"

TV cameramen and newspaper reporters were walking through the crowd. One TV reporter asked Juanita how she felt. "All tingly!" she said.

Trevor said, "I can feel my face is red!"

Then the reporter spoke to Arturo. "So, what do you get out of this park since you are leaving the school and you will soon be too big to play here?" He held a microphone up to Arturo's mouth.

Just at that minute, Arturo glimpsed Francisco walking toward him. At last! He waved wildly, jumping high so that Francisco would see him. Then he remembered the reporter with her microphone and spoke up firmly. "We got a lot out of it—"

Angel interrupted him to say, "We got to go down the slides first!"

"And we had fun doing it." Arturo wasn't going to let Angel steal his interview. "Now we know that we can do al- most anything if we try hard enough and work with other people."

Francisco stood right beside Mama and Papa and smiled proudly at Arturo. He looked almost like his old self. Arturo walked over and gave him a hug. Mama caught Arturo by the hand and whispered to him, "Lobo is in jail, and Francisco likes living in El Monte. He is going to stay with Aunt and Uncle and finish school." She looked ready to burst with joy as she squeezed Arturo's hand. She calmly took a plastic spoonful of the ice cream from the paper cup she was holding, turned to the nearby reporter, and said, "These kids have very good teachers."

But the reporter was waiting for more. "And we learned an awful lot," Arturo said, smiling because he was thinking of what Miss Fenwick had said so often and which now seemed so true. "That's the part, our teacher says, that we can take away with us."

EPILOGUE

This novel was inspired by the actions taken by thirty-five students in a California community to create a neighborhood park. Their teachers were Mary Britt and Robert Glasser.

To learn about Estrella Children's Park, the author relied on articles in the *Los Angeles Times* and the stories and scrapbooks of some of those involved.

The park is now maintained by a private endowment fund under the ownership of the "corporation" set up by the children and their teachers. It is held in trust by the California Community Foundation, a philanthropic organization, and managed at no charge by Robert Wilson.

Maintenance consists of a neighborhood resident keeping watch on the park and reporting any physical problems such as broken sprinkler heads, etc. He also mows and waters the lawn and picks up debris. For this he is paid a small salary each month. A professional landscaping service has been engaged to maintain the park. Once a year the park is thoroughly refurbished—the equipment is repainted, the lawn is resodded, new flowers and bushes are planted as needed. The endowment is earning interest, which more than covers the cost of maintenance and enables the fund to grow so that when major equipment needs to be replaced, the funds will be available.

The president of the United States sent a personal letter of congratulations to the class for this outstanding act of grassroots initiative, imagination, and hard work. The author acknowledges the class as well for inspiring her to create the fictional characters and events in this novel.

Unlike the kids in *No Place*, KAY HAUGAARD had plenty of room to play in her little country town of Malin, Oregon, with its population of only 350. In the sixth grade she hiked in the hills with her dog, Frosty, and she and her friend Barbara Ellen rode their bicycles around town, trailed by Frosty and Muffin, Barbara's wirehaired terrier. Sometimes Kay, Barbara, and Muffin rode Kay's sister's old cow pony, Billy, while Frosty trotted along beside. The girls also had great fun wading in irrigation ditches and catching pollywogs and frogs with coffee cans.

Like Arturo, Kay was interested in art and studied painting, sculpture, and art history at the University of Oregon, where she met her future husband, an architectural student. After marrying, Kay moved with her husband, Robert, to Pasadena, California, near Los Angeles—a very urban and different place from Oregon. She now teaches creative writing at Pasadena City College, where her students come from many countries and are of all colors, ages, and ethnic backgrounds. She loves the rich variety of fascinating people who, she says, "teach me more than I teach them."

Interior design by Will Powers

Typeset in Goudy Modern

by Stanton Publication Services, Inc.

Printed on acid-free 55# Sebago Antique cream paper

by Maple-Vail Book Manufacturing

If you enjoyed this book, you will also want to read these other Milkweed novels:

Gildaen, The Heroic Adventures of a Most Unusual Rabbit
BY EMILIE BUCHWALD

Chicago Tribune *Book Festival Award, Best Book for Ages 9–12*

Gildaen is befriended by a mysterious being who has lost his memory but not the ability to change shape at will. Together they accept the perilous task of thwarting the evil sorcerer, Grimald, in this tale of magic, villainy, and heroism.

The Gumma Wars
BY DAVID HAYNES

Larry "Lu" Underwood and his fellow West 7th Wildcats have been looking forward to Tony Rodriguez's birthday fiesta all year—only to discover that Lu must also spend the day with his two feuding "gummas," the name he gave his grandmothers when he was just learning to talk. The two "gummas," Gumma Jackson and Gumma Underwood, are hostile to one another, especially when it comes to claiming the affection of their only grandson. On the action-packed day of Tony's birthday, Lu, a friend, and the gummas find themselves exploring the sights of Minneapolis and St. Paul—and eventually find themselves enjoying each other's company.

Business As Usual
BY DAVID HAYNES

In Mr. Harrison's sixth-grade class, the West 7th Wildcats must learn how to run a business. Kevin Olsen, one of the Wildcats as well as the class clown, is forced out of the Wildcat group and into an unwilling alliance working in a group with the Wildcats' nemesis, Jenny Pederson. In the process of making staggering amounts of cookies for Marketplace Day, the classmates venture into the realm of free enterprise, discovering more than they imagined about business, the world, and themselves.

The Monkey Thief
BY AILEEN KILGORE HENDERSON
New York Public Library Best Books of the Year:
"Best Books for the Teen Age" Award

Twelve-year-old Steve Hanson is sent to Costa Rica for eight months to live with his uncle. There he discovers a world completely unlike anything he can see from the cushions of his couch back home, a world filled with giant trees and insects, mysterious sounds, and the constant companionship of monkeys swinging in the branches over-head. When Steve hatches a plan to capture a monkey for himself, his quest for a pet leads him into dangerous territory. It takes all of Steve's survival skills—and the help of his new friends—to get him out of trouble.

The Summer of the Bonepile Monster
BY AILEEN KILGORE HENDERSON
Milkweed Prize for Children's Literature
Alabama Library Association 1996 Juvenile/Young Adult Award

Eleven-year-old Hollis Orr has been sent to spend the summer with Grancy, his father's grandmother, in rural Dolliver, Alabama, while his parents "work things out." As summer begins, Hollis encounters a road called Bonepile Hollow, barred by a gate and a real skull and bones mounted on a board. "Things that go down that road don't ever come back," he is told. Thus begins the mystery that plunges Hollis into real danger.

I Am Lavina Cumming
BY SUSAN LOWELL
Mountains & Plains Booksellers Association Award

In 1905, ten-year-old Lavina is sent from her home on the Bosque Ranch in Arizona Territory to live with her aunt in the city of Santa Cruz, California. Armed with the Cumming family motto, "Courage," Lavina deals with a new school, homesickness, a very spoiled cousin, an earthquake, and a big decision about her future.

The Boy with Paper Wings
BY SUSAN LOWELL

Confined to bed with a viral fever, eleven-year-old Paul sails a
paper airplane into his closet and propels himself into mysterious
and dangerous realms in this exciting and fantastical adventure. Paul
finds himself trapped in the military diorama on his closet floor, out
to stop the evil commander, KRON. Armed only with paper and the
knowledge of how to fold it, Paul uses his imagination and courage
to find his way out of dilemmas and disasters.

The Secret of the Ruby Ring
BY YVONNE MACGRORY

Winner of Ireland's Bisto "Book of the Year" Award

Lucy gets a very special birthday present, a star ruby ring, from her
grandmother and finds herself transported to Langley Castle in the
Ireland of 1885. At first, she is intrigued by castle life, in which she
is the lowliest servant, until she loses the ruby ring and her only way
home.

A Bride for Anna's Papa
BY ISABEL R. MARVIN

Milkweed Prize for Children's Literature

Life on Minnesota's iron range in 1907 is not easy for thirteen-year-
old Anna Kallio. Her mother's death has left Anna to take care of the
house, her young brother, and her father, a blacksmith in the dangerous iron mines. So she and her brother plot to find their father a
new wife, even attempting to arrange a match with one of the "mail
order" brides arriving from Finland.

Minnie
BY ANNIE M. G. SCHMIDT

*Winner of the Netherlands' Silver Pencil Prize
as One of the Best Books of the Year*

Miss Minnie is a cat. Or rather, she was a cat. She is now a human,
and she's not at all happy to be one. As Minnie tries to find and

reverse the cause of her transformation, she brings her reporter friend, Mr. Tibbs, news from the cats' gossip hotline—including revealing information that one of the town's most prominent citizens is not the animal lover he appears to be.

The Dog with Golden Eyes
BY FRANCES WILBUR

Milkweed Prize for Children's Literature

Many girls dream of owning a dog of their own, but Cassie's wish for one takes an unexpected turn in this contemporary tale of friendship and growing up. Thirteen-year-old Cassie is lonely, bored, and feeling friendless when a large, beautiful dog appears one day in her suburban backyard. Cassie wants to adopt the dog, but as she learns more about him, she realizes that she is, in fact, caring for a full-grown Arctic wolf. As she attempts to protect the wolf from urban dangers, Cassie discovers that she possesses strengths and resources she never imagined.

Behind the Bedroom Wall
BY LAURA E. WILLIAMS

Milkweed Prize for Children's Literature

It is 1942. Thirteen-year-old Korinna Rehme is an active member of her local *Jungmädel*, a Nazi youth group, along with many of her friends. Korinna's parents, however, secretly are members of an underground group providing a means of escape to the Jews of their city and are, in fact, hiding a refugee family behind the wall of Korinna's bedroom. As Korinna comes to know the family, and their young daughter, her sympathies begin to turn. But when someone tips off the Gestapo, loyalties are put to the test and Korinna must decide in what she believes and whom she trusts.

MILKWEED EDITIONS publishes with the intention of making a humane impact on society, in the belief that literature is a transformative art uniquely able to convey the essential experiences of the human heart and spirit.

To that end, Milkweed publishes distinctive voices of literary merit in handsomely designed, visually dynamic books, exploring the ethical, cultural, and esthetic issues that free societies need continually to address.

Milkweed Editions is a not-for-profit press.